An Accidental Affair

An Accidental Affair

Nora Naish

ROBERT HALE · LONDON

ISBN 0 7090 7156 6

Robert Hale Limited
Clerkenwell House
Clerkenwell Green
London EC1R 0HT

2 4 6 8 10 9 7 5 3

Typeset in 11/17pt Palatino
by Derek Doyle & Associates in Liverpool.
Printed in Great Britain by
St Edmundsbury Press Ltd, Bury St Edmunds, Suffolk.
Bound by Woolnough Bookbinding Ltd.

Permission has been granted by A.P. Watt Ltd on behalf of Michael Yeats to quote from *For Anne Gregory* taken from the *Collected Poems of WB Yeats*.

Permission has been granted to quote from *The Unicorn* by Iris Murdoch, published by Chatto and Windus.

For Jenny, who knows that most of us make do with second-best.

Acknowledgements

I want to thank Maxine Balls, Major James Balls, 22nd Cheshire Regiment, and Major Peter Balls, Royal Green Jackets, for information on military details, R.A. Naish, Bob Ruthven and A. Woolley for help with other research, and all those who have encouraged me to write this novel.

1

Perhaps Ben lunched rather too well and not altogether wisely that Sunday at the Maybush up on the Mount. Certainly he drank two if not three glasses of good red French country wine. There was no reason why he shouldn't. He was not driving. Celia had taken the car, as she did every Sunday, and had driven the children to their grandparents in the Sussex stockbroker belt. The kids loved it because of the heated swimming-pool in the garden and Granny's old-fashioned Sunday roast lunch. Well, there was no harm in their tasting a bit of high life in Sussex. That was something they'd never get much of on his salary, supplemented by Celia's part-time earnings, quite apart from her dislike of the fleshpots of Egypt, of cooking in general if truth were told. She was in fact vegetarian. He rather relished the fleshpots himself, so on Sundays when he'd done his stint of organ-playing for High Mass at St Augustine's, followed by his short session of brisk jogging across the common, he felt a good lunch was what he deserved. And Toni, the proprietor of the Maybush, who was famous for his Sunday lunches, (tip-top, as Ben's father would have put it) usually talked to his customers. He was so friendly and full of jokes and happy clichés, which after the second glass sounded like the wisest of aphorisms, that Ben always felt wiser and happier for hearing them. But that particular Sunday in June when, bathed in this good-food-and-wine-and-fellowship glow, he emerged into the open air he was aware that the sky overhead was menacing. He could only suppose that a summer thunderstorm was about to break, so he hurried downhill towards the station. It was a mere five-minute walk but as he hurried there was a flash of lightning. He counted what he thought was six seconds before thunder rolled. And then the rain fell, and he realized he had no umbrella. He must have left it at the Maybush. That didn't worry him as he knew the staff would keep it for him till next Sunday. He began to run past the row of Edwardian houses at the bottom of the hill.

A very fat woman was approaching, and now the heavens opened and the rain positively pissed down. He could see there was insufficient space for two people abreast on the pavement when the second was so enormously fat, so he stepped out of her path. Unfortunately some lout had dropped a piece of slimy litter which made his foot slide as he trod on it, and he fell, twisting his ankle over the pavement's edge. He didn't groan aloud, as his tip-top father had brought him up to be stoical, but he swore loudly instead; and the fat woman, offended by his lewd language, waddled on, leaving him alone on his hands and knees in the gutter of a street now deserted even by passing cars. His clothes were getting soaked and his ankle was swelling rapidly. He tried to rise but the pain was so excruciating he knew he couldn't walk. It occurred to him that help must be available in the respectable Edwardian houses, so he crawled across the pavement and up a stone-flagged path to a front door of solid mahogany, and by leaning on it managed to drag himself upright and ring the bell, hoping that some nice, kind, motherly housewife would open it and then allow him to use her telephone to order a taxi. Through the closed door he could hear recorded music. Elgar. He recognized the *Enigma Variations*. Impossible not to, since they were so frequently broadcast on radio as to have become as hackneyed as the national anthem. He pushed the briefcase containing his sheets of music against the door hoping it might allay, by conferring on him a degree of professionalism, any fears of strange men the hoped-for housewife might have.

The door was opened by a young man. Even in the distress Ben was suffering, which he would later describe to Celia as 'dire', he couldn't help noticing how beautiful the young man was, with close-cropped black hair, bright blue eyes, and a lean, lithe body. With one glance from those unblinking eyes he recognized Ben's plight.

'I'm sorry to barge in like this,' Ben began to apologize, 'but I wonder if I might use your phone?'

'Sure,' the young man said. Putting a strong arm under Ben's elbow he heaved him over the threshold and called commandingly: 'Mum!'

Almost at once down the stairs came a woman who, apart from looking too young to be the young man's mother, proved to be all that Ben had hoped for. She made him remove his wet clothes, gave him her son's dressing-gown to wrap round himself, told him to sit down in an old stick-backed chair in the kitchen, and made him drink a cup of tea with a couple of aspirins.

13

Then she took from her freezer a packet of frozen peas, which she used as a cold compress on his ankle.

'Are you a nurse?' he asked.

'No,' she replied, 'but I once did a Red Cross first aid course. How did you do this? Were you running for a train?'

'No, I did my jogging earlier, which reminds me – oh damn and blast! – I've left my jogging togs in the church!' Things had obviously begun to slide out of control even before he drank Toni's good red wine. He sighed. It was just an unlucky day.

'Jude's got to get back to his unit. Otherwise he'd drive you home,' she said.

'Oh no, really! I wouldn't dream . . . you've been wonderfully kind already. You like Elgar?' *Nimrod* had come to an end on the CD. 'No. I'll get a taxi.'

She was sitting at his feet absent-mindedly massaging his ankle and thinking that a church was a strange place in which to leave 'jogging togs'.

'Elgar? Yes, of course. He's so English, so Edwardian really. I always think he's so right for my house, don't you see?'

Ben didn't see; he thought it a peculiar reason for liking a composer; but he was so pleasantly soothed by her gentle hand pressures around his aching joint and relieved too of pain as the aspirin began to work on him, that he simply closed his eyes and was silent.

'I think you ought to have this X-rayed, you know,' she said.

He was suddenly brought back to face reality. 'Oh no!' he protested. 'All that waiting around in the casualty department at St Barnabas! I couldn't face it. I'd better get home. My GP lives quite near me. I'm sure he wouldn't mind dropping in to take a look at it.'

'Well, if you think so . . .' She seemed doubtful.

The young man, Jude, who was a decisive person with little time to watch this small idyll of peace and kindliness, and who in any case had been about to leave the house, said:

'Well, I can't hang about much longer. Shall I ring for a taxi?' As he was dialling he spoke to Ben over his shoulder: 'You can borrow the dressing-gown.'

Ben felt rather offended when later that day Dr Corrigan made light of his injury, pooh-poohing the idea that he might need an X-ray, assuring him that the pain and swelling would all subside in a few days and that he'd be as right as rain in a week.

'No bones broken. Not a Pott's fracture at all,' he declared as he bound up Ben's right ankle and foot firmly with elastoplast, and later over a glass of whisky elaborated: 'What you've done is to rupture the big fan-like muscle over the top of your foot which extends, that is, pulls your toes up towards your nose. It will all be black and blue in the morning and will look much worse than it really is.'

'Well, it's damned painful, whatever it is,' grumbled Ben; and seeing the doctor was unperturbed by his suffering he added: 'You don't really care – do you Patrick? – unless a patient's dying.'

'I have so many dying patients,' said Corrigan. 'I confess the rest do sometimes seem to me to be rather small fry.' He had been trained in Dublin and had not emigrated to London and the Home Counties till the seventies. He still retained his Irish brogue, and a certain softness that went with it. He was easy-going; he believed in letting things be, in not interfering too much, in waiting and seeing, and for the most part, since he was rarely called on to deal with accidents or emergencies, his practice worked. It was true that he attended a hospice for the dying as well as an up-market old people's home, which in his own mind he called 'God's Waiting-room'; and it seemed to him that most people were so healthy nowadays they didn't need much medical attention till their last years when the mechanism simply wore out and fell to bits. And for that he had no miracle cure inside his medical bag of tricks, nothing more than a kindly word for the surviving relatives. Most of his time nowadays seemed to be used up in attempting to reassure healthy persons scared out of their common sense by the fear of contracting some extremely rare disease improperly understood but nevertheless widely broadcast for the sake of media kicks.

'Get moving on it as soon as you can,' he said. 'And don't try to drive until you're sure you can use the brake.' He rose from his chair. 'No. Don't move old chap. I'll see myself out. Stay where you are. My love to Celia when she gets back. And tell her not to worry about you.'

Celia showed more concern than Dr Corrigan. She fussed about preparing him a hot drink which he didn't want, removing from him the dressing-gown and throwing it into the washing-machine when it didn't need washing, and uttering little exclamations of alarm as he crawled on all fours up to bed; and he was grateful for a tender loving care she was usually too busy to show.

'Have you broken a bone, Daddy?' asked Chris hopefully. He was seven. Sarah, who at ten was already showing a tendency towards philosophizing, remarked as she watched Ben's progress:

'Crawling's very slow compared to walking.'

An Accidental Affair

Next day when he found himself alone in the house, the children safely in their comprehensive school and Celia on her way to her sixth form college where she taught French, he noticed how quiet it was. Everybody got out of Bushbridge in the morning; it was simply a place where people slept; it was only at weekends that it came to life with lawnmowing and neighbours talking to each other over fences, and children running in and out of each other's gardens. He knew he was going to be terribly bored. It was too painful to walk even with the aid of an old walking-stick of his father's which Celia had fished out of the back of a cupboard; he would have to stay indoors. He should, he thought, send some expression of gratitude to those kind people who had helped him yesterday. He remembered the handsome boy vividly, but could hardly recall the mother apart from an image of a mass of brown hair hanging over his foot, and her pretty hands. He knew the name of the street in which the house stood: Alexandra Row, and now that he thought about it he could see the number above the doorbell he had rung: Number 11. Flowers, he thought. That would be the thing. He could send flowers by phone through Marlene, the florist down in the village. But how would he address the recipient? He tried to remember whether or not those pretty hands had worn a wedding ring. He didn't think so. But that didn't mean much these days. There had been no father in the house during his brief visit as far as he could see; but there had undoubtedly been a father once. Best to address her as Ms he decided. Miz. That might annoy her if she was married; and anyway Miz What? The solution came to him at last. He would send roses, not red roses

17

which spoke of love, nor white lilies which might suggest a death, but a bouquet of simple garden flowers unmixed with any complicated associations; and he would address his gift to *Enigma Variations, 11 Alexandra Row, Milton*. That would take her by surprise. He laughed softly as he lifted the phone and dialled Marlene's High Class Florists: Weddings and Funerals and Interflora a Speciality.

The arrival of the bouquet sheathed in a cone of polythene and tied with ribbon bows and twists did indeed cause a very pleasant surprise. The donor's name, it seemed, was Ben Fording. *Sprained ankle only. From a grateful patient with thanks.* What a nice man, Letty thought, and a good thing it was only a sprain, not a fracture! All the same that painful ankle would stop his jogging for a bit. She smiled, thinking of those jogging togs languishing in some church for several weeks before he'd be fit enough to pick them up. So it was an even greater surprise when on the following Sunday she answered a ring at the front door and came face to face with him again. She noticed that he had a walking-stick in his hand. He noticed that she was wearing an apron over jeans.

This time it was not Elgar reverberating through the hall but Mendlessohn's *Fingal's Cave* sending runs of rippling water and echoes of Scottish folk-songs into the air.

'I couldn't ring up first,' he explained. 'I don't know your name, you know.'

She smiled, wiping her hands on her apron.

'It's Laetitia,' she said. 'I'm not an Enigma at all. Letty for short.'

'Oh!' he said. 'How nice. Laetitia is joy – better than Felicity, which is mere happiness.'

She said nothing, but stood smiling stupidly and thinking: What a precise old buffer he is! But not old really, since his hair is not at all grey.

He handed her a parcel. 'It's the dressing-gown you lent me. And I wondered if I might take you out to lunch at the Maybush. It's where I usually go on Sundays.'

'Oh!' she said. 'How lovely! But the Maybush is rather posh. I'll have to change, won't I? Do come inside. I've got the clothes you left – all nicely aired. And thank you for the flowers. Much appreciated.'

She turned and began to walk away, and as she did so he saw that she was limping. It seemed an extraordinary coincidence, and for a moment he wondered if she too could have sprained her ankle, but as he watched he noticed she wasn't limping so much as dragging her right leg.

When he looked up his eyes met the hostile stare of a weather-beaten old man who was stepping into the hall from the bright rectangle of sunshine of the garden beyond.

'This is Barney,' said Letty over her shoulder. 'We grow the vegetables together.' She waved an introductory hand. 'Show him the garden, Barney, while I go up and change.'

'Morning,' said Barney, but without a smile.

It was a surprisingly large garden for a terraced house in Alexandra Row for the simple reason that the three plots belonging to Numbers 10, 11 and 12 had all been merged into one communal open space by the removal of their fences. Barney's area, Number 10, was the vegetable garden, Letty's provided a central lawn with a spectacular giant rosebush which concealed her patch of raspberry canes beyond.

'Mrs Crinkham's on the right,' explained Barney. 'She grows

the strawberries at the bottom of the garden. But we won't go down there as she'll have her binoculars trained on you.' He didn't explain why his neighbour should want to examine Ben so closely, but continued: 'She can't see us if we stand inside the loggia.' This was a sort of pergola outside the back door around which fell in profusion the long yellow tassels of laburnum.

'Spectacular rose, that,' said Ben. 'I've never seen one like that before.'

'It's *Rosa Nevada*,' said Barney. His face assumed a dreamy, worshipping look. 'It's a wonderful rose all right. And Letty's favourite.'

Ben could tell by the softness with which he spoke her name what Barney felt about her. He was a retired electrician whose craft had trained him to be logical. He believed in reason and the solving of problems by means of it. Reason could not however move mountains; he knew that. Moreover he feared, especially since the death of his wife in her sixties from cancer, the hostility of the Fates, and allowed himself no hubris. He never boasted, nor let his expectations grow great for fear of inevitable disappointment. His two sons had left home, one to work in Saudi Arabia, the other in Canada, so he was alone in Number 10 Alexandra Row when he retired. His long love affair with Letty had begun over the intervening fence. It was there that they had conceived the idea of a communal garden; and since he had plenty of unaccustomed leisure while she was out at work all day, he had undertaken the removal of fences and the laying-out of garden beds. Mrs Crinkham on the other side was meanwhile being plied with persuasion by Letty, and it was not long before she too joined the scheme.

'But that rose,' Barney said, checking his own praise of it lest the Fates in the shape of garden pests, fungi, sudden frosts or vandalism might through sheer jealousy blemish its beauty, 'it does only have one month of flowering. So you're lucky to see it. It's not a good repeating hybrid. And it's too large for this garden. It needs a park really to show it off.' Ben's unstinted admiration for the rose had entirely melted Barney's initial wariness.

Letty came downstairs as Mendelessohn's music ended. She was wearing a sea-green silk trouser suit and wore a necklace of heavy amber beads. 'Fetching' was how Ben's father would have described her. Part of Ben's heart sank at sight of her. The fact was he didn't want to be fetched. He was, after all, married to a good kind wife, and was the father of two lovely children. Romantic complication was the last thing he needed in his life. The other part of his heart was suddenly lifted as he thought: Laetitia. Joy. She was a sea-nymph floating down the stairs, drifting towards him out of Fingal's Cave, emerging from the shadowed mouth of it and from the clutches of Fingal the Celtic warrior, a macho monster to whom she had no doubt been in thrall, but now, shimmering with light reflected from her sea-green mermaid's body, and from the chain of sunshine flickering round her neck, she was escaping into the silence following the closing bars, and was about to have lunch with him at the Maybush. Sometimes the sound of familiar music did fill his head with fantasies.

For a moment he hesitated, wondering if she'd be able to make it up the hill with that weak leg of hers. Then without a word he took her arm, and together they began the climb.

Toni took them up to the first floor and seated them by his special picture-window overlooking the windy common. He was hovering a bit, Ben thought. He could see Toni was delighted at the advent of this charming new customer. In fact Toni was just a bit anxious as well as curious, wondering who she might be, for of course he knew Mr Fording was a married man with two lovely kids whose holiday faces he'd seen in snapshots many times over the years. As he poured out their anticipatory glasses of Soave before what was to be an all-Italian lunch he surveyed the strange green lady with an expert eye and decided that she was safe. Charming, but no longer young, a kind, serious woman, but no destroying angel; a certain off-beat beauty, yes, but certainly no sex kitten. With a little sigh of relief he judged that Mr Fording would be OK.

Meanwhile Letty, unaware of the scrutiny she was being subjected to, had discovered that Ben was the organist at St Augustine's on Milton Mount, the Victorian Gothic church built at the same time as the Independent School for Boys, when High Anglicanism was at its zenith. It was why, Ben explained, the music department was so well endowed it could afford to employ him as well as his old friend Father Gregory, who was director of music at the school and master of the choir at the church. It was why the full panoply of a sung high mass was maintained every Sunday here, unlike its Roman Catholic counterpart, which now provided only an evening low mass for worshippers returning from their weekends away.

'They have moved with the times for the greater convenience of their parishioners,' said Ben, adding: 'We're still singing.' He was lucky, he explained. 'I don't play to an empty church. You see the whole school has to attend Sunday high mass, all the boys, and the teachers, and then there are usually a few parents as well as the occasional local parishioner. So I have a full house.'

Between the church and the school was a sports complex complete with shower-rooms, and as these were empty on Sundays Father Gregory permitted his old friend the use of a shower after the physical exercise he took following high mass. Last Sunday after showering he had returned to the church to pick up the briefcase that he'd left beside the organ, and it was then that he'd mislaid those jogging togs.

Ben discovered to his surprise and pleasure that Letty's father had been no other than John Cresswell, head of the Mountside Music Academy, where often in the past Ben had put through their paces young musicians, pianists, violinists, and the occasional organist, all struggling to pass the examinations set by LUMCA. He had been very sorry when old Cresswell died. He was so fond of him. Everybody was. And the Academy had flourished under his headship.

'Amazingly,' said Letty. 'I never could understand how. He couldn't make a decision, you know. But all the lady teachers and secretaries adored him, and did everything for him. I believe it was they who ran the place. He merely signed on the dotted line.'

Ben was surprised by this revelation about Cresswell. He sipped his Soave and looked at Letty across the table.

'What a marvellous view!' she said. She was sitting facing the big window, and the light fell on her face and on her thick brown hair. Her green eyes gazed with rapt attention across grassy spaces dotted with Sunday walkers and their dogs to the distant horizon. 'I wonder if there are still skylarks on the common nowadays?' she said.

He was aware of a not altogether pleasant fluttering in his stomach and took another sip of Soave to steady his nerves. A thread of notes began to spiral through his mind's ear

'The Lark Ascending,' he said. 'Vaughan Williams lived in deepest Gloucestershire. There would have been plenty of larks there. Too many walkers on the common for larks to nest now.'

She took her eyes off the view with an effort and looked at him. 'You're fond of Vaughan Williams ?'

'Lyricism. Yes,' he replied. 'What about you? Who are your favourite composers?'

'Oh, Chopin, Rachmaninov and Puccini,' she said without hesitation.

He considered her over the rim of his glass. She was an out-and-out romantic, he thought. She must know the pain of loss, and perhaps was still yearning for love.

'And you?'

'Impossible to choose from so many Greats. But perhaps Schubert and Mahler.'

'Lovely wine,' she said, sipping and thinking: He thinks of suffering, and fears death.

'But I suppose really in the end Beethoven is God,' he said, and laughed. 'When I was a small boy learning the piano I adored Beethoven. I thought of him as some sort of saint. And when I made a mess of a bar, or played a wrong note I used to pray to him, asking him to forgive my ham-fistedness. I actually believed, when I was ten, in the Communion of Saints! – that the church militant on earth could commune by prayer with the church triumphant in heaven.' She laughed too, wondering how much of a Christian he still was. 'Jude . . .' he said speculatively. 'Why Jude?'

'I was reading Hardy all the time I was expecting him,' she explained. *'Jude the Obscure.* I felt then that my baby and I belonged to the great army of the obscure.'

'You weren't happy?'

'Well, I'd been deserted by his father. I was a single parent with a very uncertain future to look forward to. His father decided to hitch-hike round the world just about the time when Jude was travelling into it. But Pa – that's John Cresswell to you – looked after us both. So it's all worked out more or less.'

'Much more than less I should say,' Ben's expansive Sunday mood was overtaking him. 'You've brought up a marvellous young man, haven't you?'

'Do you think so?' Her sweet sad face broke into such a radiant smile that Ben's heart suddenly took off like Shelley's skylark and rose into unpremeditated rejoicing as the lasagne arrived smelling deliciously of all sorts of herbs, needing Chianti, Ben insisted, to go with it.

'I was a fiercely protective mother,' she said. 'But Jude didn't want protection. He soon threw it off to become a warrior.' She laughed, remembering how Pa's overgrown garden became Jude's jungle full of wild beasts and dangerous enemies to hunt, with neighbouring children acting out the parts he assigned to them in his armies of Crusaders and Saracens, of Cowboys and Indians. 'He was a born soldier. Funny thing, isn't it ? Genetic I suppose. His father's father was a good soldier, and was decorated for it after the battle of Arnhem.' After a pause she added: 'His father wasn't good at anything.'

'Well, he had a good eye for a female,' said Ben.

She looked up from her plate straight into his eyes and blushed. Yes, he was certainly a nice, kind man; but she didn't feel inclined to tell him about Jude's father, who had stormed into her student life in the middle of the second year of her degree course in biology. So like Jude he was: good looking, sexually persuasive, but ruthless. At the time she had loved him madly, unreasonably, without reflection or criticism. And what a fool she had been to get pregnant when at twenty she should have known better!

It was the prospect of fatherhood that had so frightened him that he'd fled. She didn't want to remember that time, those months of misery when her belly was so swollen she'd been ashamed to appear at lectures, had given up her studies altogether and stayed all day in the flat she shared with two other girls, feeling she was a failure, derelict, a cripple with a twisted leg about to bring into the world a baby whose needs she had very little idea how to meet, nor how she'd ever earn enough money to keep him. It was then that she had seen herself as one of Hardy's heroines, living in Hardy's woeful world, till one day her father phoned her:

'Why not come and live with me, Letty? Dull old place, I know, but while things are difficult, eh . . .? The child will need some sort of a father, you know – though of course I'd never interfere . . . . And I need company myself. A bit lonely, you know, since I retired . . . . Very little to do. And a big empty house.'

So her ineffectual, indecisive father, whose own wife had fled from him years ago in sheer exasperation at his hesitations, leaving Letty to become at an early age his 'little home-maker', suddenly made up his mind and set about picking up the pieces of his daughter's life and dropping them into his crumbling old house. The garden proved a wonderful nursery for Jude, with mysterious corners to explore and overgrown shrubberies to hide in before ambushing with his gang alien invaders from outer space, or the milkman, or the newspaper delivery boy. It was then, too, that Pa came into his own in a surprising way. He made bows and arrows out of twigs, and carved elegant and not too lethal daggers whose blades he painted with silver paint.

'They're made of steel,' said Jude solemnly as he gave them to his men. 'They're for hand-to-hand combat.'

To the boys Pa was some sort of magician. They called him Dagger Dog, saluting him when he walked down the garden path. One November he organized a bramble-clearing party. It was a beastly job, but they loved doing it because it entailed slashing the thorny stems, and piling them on to a bonfire. When this was blazing steadily they danced round it stamping and chanting: 'Dagger Dog! Dagger Dog! Dig, dig, dig the Dagger Dog!' It was like a scene from *Lord of the Flies*. She needed no reminding; she already knew what little boys were made of. Sometimes the knowledge frightened her; but Pa revelled in it.

It was during these years that Letty began to think of gardening, of the soil itself, and it was in that derelict garden that she began, as she put it, to see green. So in a way Pa helped to save her soul too. The background music helped of course. Although never a player herself, she liked to listen when luminaries of the Mountside Academy assembled at his house to make music. And Letty cooked supper for them. She sometimes reflected wryly on how she'd exchanged biology for cooking, but she was too busy to be bitter, and too happy watching over Jude's colourful development to be disappointed.

Toni's special Sicilian Ice-cream, a many-layered multi-coloured profusion of flavours scattered over with chopped pistachio nuts, had to be eaten in respectful silence, but afterwards over the caffè cappuccino Letty reverted to the subject of

Jude, who was never far from her thoughts.

'Naturally I agree with you about Jude. He was a gift from the gods; and I'm a very lucky woman. I know they do say mothers are partial, which I suppose is true; but all the same, yes, he is a marvellous person.'

'He looks like a soldier. Is he?'

'That's all he ever wanted to be. Colonel de la Billière has been his pin-up since he was a schoolboy, and I guess he's following in his footsteps. Jude's always being sent on some mission or other. He doesn't tell me what he's doing. I never know where he is or what he's up to, but he does come home from time to time. And that's all that matters.' Ben nodded. 'He may come home next Sunday, as we'll be having a little celebration then. Would you like to come too?'

Ben was smiling idiotically at her, his upper lip decorated with a layer of froth. She couldn't suppress a giggle.

'You've got a wonderful *mustachio bianco à la cappuccino!*' she said, proffering one of Toni's snowy napkins across the table, while Toni, who had overheard her massacre of his beautiful language, turned away shuddering.

Ben didn't feel foolish, only foolishly happy, as he took the napkin and wiped his mouth.

'Of course it might bore you,' she hesitated. 'My lunch wouldn't be anything like as grand as this one you've treated me to.'

'That's very sweet of you, Letty. Of course I'd love to come.' It wasn't, of course, Jude, but his mother he wanted to see again.

2

The perfect English summer's day is rare and therefore memorable; and this, the last Sunday in June that year was one Ben would remember all his life. No music filled the house this time, but delicious cooking smells assailed his nostrils as he followed Barney to the back porch, his birthday gift of a bottle of champagne tucked under his arm. Dappled sunshine fell through the laburnum arch on to a fat lady sitting in a wicker armchair which creaked every time she moved, and rippled over her loose black dress and the several highly coloured floating scarves she wore pinned to her bosom with a brooch of black onyx with seed pearls set in gold, that to Ben looked old and valuable. She was smoking a cigarette from a long ivory holder that had somehow survived half a century's use.

'Isadora Crinkham,' she said, proffering her left hand to Ben, who bowed over it as he placed the bottle on the table between them. 'Oh, I say! Champagne!' she cried. 'I do love a bottle of champagne at a celebration. So phallic, don't you think? All those macho rally drivers pushing it around to make a big pop, and then all the orgasmic froth exploding everywhere!'

'A bloody waste of good booze, if you ask me,' was Barney's comment.

'I'm not a rally driver. I'm a church organist,' said Ben primly.

'I suppose that *is* rather different,' said Isadora. She sounded disapppointed.

'But I'll get a good pop and try to waste as little as possible,' he promised.

Letty left the kitchen and stood beside Barney to watch the bottle-opening ritual, which was performed in silence.

'To my Birthday Girl!' said Barney, lifting his glass.

'To my Miranda, calmer of tempests!' declaimed Isadora.

'Letty!' murmured Ben, his eyes sparkling and dancing above the champagne bubbles.

'Lovely', she said, sipping. 'Thank you Ben.' She was wearing a navy-and-white-striped cook's apron over her mermaid suit.

They sat down to eat in the kitchen. Ben noticed the empty place laid for Jude. Letty explained as she carried the first dish from the stove: 'I never know with Jude. He may not turn up. Probably not today, as he's already sent me carnations with greetings. Interflora. Heaven knows where he's gone. Defusing land-mines in Africa perhaps.' She stopped, seeing the look on Ben's face. 'Yes. Of course it's dangerous; but he's very clever at what he does. And anyway I do believe he has a charmed life.'

She had cooked fresh salmon in a bouillon with onion and bay-leaf and now displayed it on a blue-and-white charger with a sprig of cress in its mouth. Barney had provided his first early potatoes and his very first broad beans of the season for the meal. Letty added a bottle of white burgundy to go with it.

'What d'you think of the spuds?' asked Barney. 'They're a new variety. Charlotte. French.'

'And none the worse for that,' said Isadora.

'Scrumptious,' said Ben.

Mrs Crinkham's contribution to the feast was a dish piled high with scarlet strawberries, and a bowl of whipped cream.

'They're marvellous!' said Ben. 'And every one seems perfect.' He remembered his own attempts in the past at growing strawberries in a patch of the back garden in Bushbridge where slugs had eaten most of his crop. 'Don't you get trouble with slugs?'

'Oh, of course, hundreds of the horrid beasts! But I trap them.'

'You use slug pellets?'

A shocked silence followed his question, shaming him into realizing how environmentally incorrect he was, till Letty kindly explained:

'We don't use pesticides, Ben. The slug pellets certainly do kill slugs; but what if birds or hedgehogs ate the poisoned slugs?'

Isadora described her traps. She called them slug pubs because they were jam jars half-filled with beer which slugs were unable to resist. 'They all die of drink,' she said with satisfaction.

'But don't the birds get drunk from eating beer-sodden slugs?' asked Ben.

'I think not,' she replied. 'Do we get drunk on eating *coq au vin*?' She smiled at him archly. 'So you're a musician? Are you a composer too?'

'My parents hoped I would be. Parents expect so much, don't they? And of course when I was a boy I imagined myself a second Arthur Rubenstein. It wasn't till I went to music college

31

and met the competition that I learned the truth: that I was a pretty second-rate thumper of the ivory keys.'

'Ah well!' sighed Isadora sympathetically. 'We all must have our dreams. "Man's reach must exceed his grasp/ Or what is heaven for?" as Browning put it somewhere.'

'I work for LUMCA,' Ben said. 'London United Music Colleges Association. I examine young musicians, as well as teaching the little blighters the piano.'

'Well then, you are one of us,' said Isadora, 'trying to maintain an oasis of civilized life in this urban cultural desert we live in.'

'Coffee outside, I think,' said Letty.

Isadora winked at Ben as she sank into her creaking chair and lit a cigarette. 'Smoking permitted in the open air,' she explained. She waved her ivory holder to demarcate the boundaries of their oasis. He could see that the fence at the bottom of the gardens was surmounted by barbed wire.

'We had to put it up to stop the thieves and vandals from beyond the alleyway,' said Barney.

'Once a right-of-way between the fields that used to be there,' said Letty. 'Before it was all built over.'

'Prole Alley now,' said Isadora. 'Beyond it lies Animal Farm. Almost what Orwell led us to expect. Big Brother among media moguls, Head Pig of the ruling swine, keeps them happy with the hogwash he pours into the dishes they put out for it on their rooftops.'

'Do they try to steal the vegetables?' asked Ben.

'Those sorts of people don't eat vegetables,' said Isadora. 'They live on bread and pig fat with a few canned fizzy drinks thrown in. What they steal is my strawberries.'

'Doesn't the barbed wire keep them out?'

'I keep them out. I'm the watchperson here.' She took from a pocket in her voluminous gown a pair of opera glasses, and began to peer through them. 'I do believe there's that flasher at it again. I can only see his head; but I know him by the pink bobble on his woolly hat.'

'Well, if I catch him I'll empty a bucket of horse manure over his woolly hat,' said Barney.

'That would be a waste of good manure,' Letty objected. 'And where, may I ask, did you manage to get it?'

'From the riding-stables up on the Mount.'

'I could do with some for my *Rosa Nevada*,' said Letty.

'Oh, he does no harm,' interrupted Isadora. 'The flasher's only showing off what's there. And if people haven't seen it before, it's high time they did. But there's a blackbird, Barney, pecking at stuff on your compost heap.'

'He'll do no harm. He's no vandal,' said Barney.

'He is when he attacks my strawberry bed,' she retorted. 'But he's not as bad as the kids from over the other side.' What she meant was the other side of the alleyway that ran along the bottom of their gardens, dividing them from the area where small houses, crowded with children and pets, huddled together in a noisy, disorderly struggle for survival for life in the underclass. 'They swarm, you know – the kids. Birth control doesn't seem to have trickled down to income groups four and five, any more than the promised wealth.'

'I can see you're busy,' said Ben.

'Oh, I'm never bored. I have too many enemies. I'm the watchwoman here, you see. Barney uses my patch for vegetables, Letty grows raspberries. I keep watch over it all,' She waved her cigarette-holder dismissively, knocking over her coffee-cup.

'Oh dear!' cried Ben. 'Can I help?'

Letty was already running to the kitchen for a cloth to wipe the black fluid from the table.

'A little water cleans us of this deed,' said Isadora airily, heaving her bulk out of the armchair. 'I won't overstay my welcome. I am the very pink of courtesy. And I won't offer to help with the washing-up, as Barney does it so much better than I do.'

He threw her a glance that was far from kind, but he picked up the tray with its crockery, and took it to the kitchen.

'It's a sort of *commune à trois* you have here,' said Ben, following Letty along a path between her plot and Barney's.

'We help each other and so help ourselves. It's as simple as that. We enjoy a quality of life we wouldn't otherwise. We could never afford to buy the beautiful asparagus Barney grows on Isadora's patch.' She stopped beside a rosebush to squeeze greenfly from a bud and snip off a few deadheads with the secateurs she carried. 'I'm the only one who's earning a salary, courtesy of the Inland Revenue, three stops down the line.'

'You don't look like an income-tax inspector.'

'I'm a revenue officer. Not everybody's friend. I look into the profits of small businesses. But my neighbours here, who are both retired, have time and plenty of energy still.'

'Mrs Crinkham is a great talker,' said Ben.

'You mean: Doesn't she get on my nerves? She likes declaiming, so I let her talk. I like listening to her. It's as good as going to the theatre. She was an actress when she was young, you know. Repertory. That's why she's always quoting – mostly Shakespeare. She adores the bard.' She stooped to wipe her green-stained fingers on the grass before dipping them into the rainwater in a butt that drained Barney's greenhouse roof. 'We're lucky to have this water for the garden,' she said. 'Although it doesn't look as if we're all going to suffer from intermittent water shortage yet.'

'I suppose she's fairly well off?'

'Oh, no, she's quite poor. She owns her house, but has only her old-age pension. How she manages I don't know. I suspect she does a bit of small antiques dealing now and again. She's pretty shrewd.'

Beyond Barney's greenhouse, where he 'brought on' his seedlings prior to planting them out, stood a damson tree, its dark fruits beginning to swell. Letty stood admiring it.

'I make damson jam,' she said. 'It's such a treat later in the year.'

He was tempted to put an arm round her waist, but resisted the impulse, fearing Isadora's binoculars on his back. She lingered, guessing his desire, wanting to encourage him but not knowing exactly how.

When they reached the *Rosa Nevada* she stopped for a moment to examine its long stems, heavily laden with big creamy flowers, and then, fearless of its thorns, she pushed her way into the great bush and quickly cut off all the deadheads within reach. Ben watched her as she emerged, trying to free her greensleeved arms from the entanglement of branches. For a moment he saw her transfigured in the bright light, as if crowned with the brutal thorns of her great rose, while blossoms adorned her hair; she was the apotheosis of that summer afternoon, the nymph-goddess of her garden, half-rooted like Daphne in the soil, whose fingers turned into bay-leaves as she fled to escape the embraces of Apollo the god.

He was filled with a leaden feeling of regret as he took the secateurs from her hand. Ah, Letty, Letty . . . Why didn't I stand here like this with you before today? Why didn't we meet years ago when I was free to love you? It might have been, could have been, would have been the perfect marriage.

His sadness persisted as they walked back to the house, pausing to observe Isadora's strawberries and the asparagus bed on the way. He glanced up at her windows, wondering if she sat there watching them.

On the table under the laburnum arch two parcels, birthday presents wrapped in pretty paper, had been left by the departing guests. One was a book from Barney, the other a new CD of Gershwin songs from Isadora. While Letty slipped the CD into her player, Ben picked up the book and flipped over its pages. Barney must have found it in a second-hand bookshop, for it was a rather battered old edition of one of Darwin's lesser-known works: *The Formation of Vegetable Mould through the Action of Worms*. Under the title, in smaller print, Ben read: *With Observations on their Habits*.

'I say Letty, just listen to this,' he called out as the first notes of piano jazz sounded from the hall.

' "Worms do not possess any sense of hearing . . . When placed on a table close to the keys of a piano, which was played as loudly as possible, they remained perfectly quiet. Although indifferent to undulations in the air audible by us, they are extremely sensitive to vibrations in any solid object".'

She sat down to listen to his reading, while he with half an ear heard the recorded piano play the melody of *Lady be Good*, and murmured: 'Unforgettable – Gershwin!'

'Go on,' she said.

' "When the pots containing two worms which had remained quite indifferent to the sound of the piano, were placed *on* this instrument, and the note C in the bass clef was struck, both instantly retreated into their burrows. After a time they emerged, and when G above the line in the treble clef was struck they again retreated". What do you think of that?'

'They haven't got ears to hear with,' she said. 'So I suppose they must feel vibrations through their skins.'

'Surprising, isn't it?'

They were silent as the music changed to *Someone to Watch over Me*, and a dark, sexy voice caught and held their attention. It made Ben anxious. He thought: I ought to go. He stood up and stammered awkwardly:

'I think . . . it's been wonderful, Letty. Perhaps . . .'

She stood up, and for a moment faced him before he suddenly put his arms round her, groaning softly:

'Oh Letty, Letty . . .' while the dusky voice like a hot soldering iron, ran through them, fusing them together. *Someone to watch over me*. When Ben released her and stumbled off across the hall towards the front door, she watched him go without a word.

He made his way automatically towards the station, almost unaware of where he was going, or what he was doing, so blinded was he by the confusion of his thoughts and feelings. Like the earthworms, he told himself, we too may feel, in a vibration of the flesh, the music of the spheres. I must be in love, he thought, shocked by the discovery. It was a state of being he'd almost forgotten; he had lived for so long a safe, suburban existence of routine work and small pleasures, had accepted so long ago the inevitable disappointments of married life, the loss of bliss, and had been thankful at least for the dull contentment of it, finding solace in his work, and an occasional thrill on hearing a phrase of music or a song well sung.

I do believe, he reflected, as he produced his season ticket before stepping on to the platform, I do believe it was that wretched song. He shook his head irritably, but the thing insinuated itself into the ear of memory, wouldn't leave him alone. *Someone to watch over me.* Love was dangerous, wasn't it? It could be a destructive fire, obliterating years of work, turning to ashes the foundations of everything he had relied on, family life as well as moral principles, everything he held dear. Good heavens! Somehow he'd been an awful fool.

Why hadn't he seen this coming before, and taken avoiding action? It wasn't as if he was a teenager falling helplessly into a Romeo and Juliet affair. And that hadn't ended exactly happily, had it? He sat down and stared across the carriage at an advert for a herbal pill promising to enhance male potency. That was something he could do without just now. And then another voice inside him began to argue, making excuses for him. This love he'd fallen into was as accidental as his fall in the rain-sodden street a few weeks ago, when he had stumbled into a little Eden hidden behind the terraced façade of Alexandra Row and had been entranced by some sort of summer madness, had been overwhelmed by – yes, why not admit it? – desire for this woman, for her cool mermaid's body, and her sweet caressing hands.

Letty, Letty, Letty ... he could hear inside his head as the wheels of the train clicked over the track. Why shouldn't he love her, and be loved by her? Surely a man was entitled to at least one great passionate love affair in his lifetime? He would be an idiot to repudiate this offer from the gods. He remembered Shelley's words, inscribed by Elgar at the beginning of his Symphony in E flat: *Rarely, rarely, comest thou, Spirit of Delight*. If he didn't seize it now it might slip out of his grasp for ever.

On Monday afternoon, in between listening to the few piano pupils he taught in Bushbridge, he walked out into his garden and surveyed his property: a redbrick neo-Georgian detached house on Balmoral Drive on the newly 'developed' estate. He looked at his own front door, and at the climbing roses on either side of it. They were meagre and straggling now, due to neglect, but he remembered when he'd bought them with Celia at the garden centre, how enthusiastic they'd been, imagining the crimson blooms of Dublin Bay growing up on one side, while pure-white climbing Iceberg flowered on the other. He remembered digging holes for them, tamping down the soil around the roots and happily thinking: roses round the door promised happiness. Sarah had been a toddler then, patting the earth solemnly with her little hands around his boots, and Chris had been but a baby cooing in his carrycot on the newly sown lawn. Celia was still a mum proud to be at home. She had not yet gone back to her college job.

The thought of his children made him swallow suddenly. How could he allow his imagination to dwell on Letty, he asked himself, when he knew very well that if he didn't check the crazy passion that was invading his soul he could be swept away from this anchorage, from his past, could be carried away, drowning in the flood, while on the distant bank his children stood calling out to him? He could hear in his mind Smetana's

Ma Vlast, the great broad river roaring in his ears as it carried him further and further downstream, and in the distance his children were crying. No. He could not, must not let this happen.

His firm determination held all that week, and the next, and was strong throughout his session at the organ on the following Sunday, though he found, during the jolly music he usually played at the end of high mass to signal to the congregation that it was time to go, and before he was quite aware of what was happening, a small anarchic melody creeping into his improvisation: *Someone to watch over me*. And for a moment he feared he might lose control of the keys; but he managed to pull his wits together. This should be dismissal music. He didn't want people to linger in the aisles in a trance. A bit of discreetly jazzed up Brandenburg was needed to pepper their departure.

Letty was disappointed when she heard nothing from Ben all that week. She thought it strange that there was no letter from him, no phone call, and stranger still when next Sunday came and went without a sign from him. After that she felt sad, and a little bitter. She guessed he must be married, like all the other men she'd fancied in recent years, or afraid, for one reason or another, of getting involved. Well, I've lived alone a long time now, she told herself; I should be used to it. Most of the time she didn't mind; but there had been days, especially since Jude had left home, when she felt lonely. During the week she was too busy at work to think about her feelings much; and when she got home, by the time she'd cooked herself a meal, chatted to Barney and Isadora if they were out and about, and done a few jobs in the garden while the summer twilight slowly faded, and finally had sunk gratefully into a hot bath, she was ready to fall asleep, which she did rapidly. She had always slept well, and believed it was this faculty which had saved her sanity in the past, and now kept her going.

On Sundays there was always lunch to cook for her neighbours and partners in the garden venture, always news to exchange and plans to discuss. But on Saturdays when she pushed her trolley round the supermarket aisles to buy food and household goods for the coming week, she sometimes caught herself gazing blankly at an ecologically correct label on a packet without reading it, because she was fantasizing about some nice-looking man she'd seen near the ethnic foods shelves, and was in imagination far away, holding the stranger's hand as they strolled along a Mediterranean beach, or ran together into the sea, where they splashed each other and laughed like children. The shock of the price tag on the packet usually brought her back to reality with a sharp slap. Good heavens! Just how corny can your dreams be? she would reprove herself.

The few attractive men she'd actually met in recent years had all proved to be either of the romantic vagrant variety with an itch to move on after a few weeks' acquaintance, or securely married men too heavily mortgaged to risk more than a little light adultery. But she knew Ben was different. He had expressed wordlessly, with look and gesture in all sorts of subliminal ways that he wanted her, and needed her, and as soon as he held her in his arms that Sunday she knew he loved and longed for her. She knew, too, that he was unhappy; she recognized her own need to care for him; she felt intuitively that this was love, the real thing, which up to now had always eluded her.

By the second Saturday after her birthday she found herself dawdling near the phone; and when it rang she jumped, dropping the receiver, and then spoke hurriedly and eagerly to a surprised voice trying to sell her an unwanted conservatory to be delivered to the house in ready-made modules. By Sunday, when she knew she was going to be alone for once, as Barney had gone off to a cycling club reunion in Painter's Park, and Isadora had been taken off by a dutiful niece to Hampton Court for the day, Letty decided to waylay Ben as he walked down to the station after lunching at Toni's.

She timed it fairly accurately. She put a CD on the recorder in the hall and opened the upstairs windows overlooking the street. Just before 3 p.m. as she sat by Jude's bedroom window at the front of the house she saw him coming down the hill. He was looking rather mournful, she thought, staring at his feet as he walked; but when he approached Number 11 he glanced up at the front door, and seemed to hesitate for a moment. Letty, shrinking behind the curtain, her heart beating very fast, hoped he would walk up the garden path and ring the bell. But he turned and walked on.

Immediately she leaned out of the window and called out: 'Hullo Ben! Aren't you coming in?'

He turned back and looked up at her with a troubled expression, and then smiled slowly.

'Letty,' he said. 'Is it really you?'

'Wait a minute,' she said. 'I'll come down at once.' I'm being immoral, she thought, tempting him into Number 11, seducing him with Prokofiev's music, when his conscience is doing its best to push him home to the wife and family she guessed he must have, but I don't care. She tossed her hair back as she opened the door.

42

'I thought you had forgotten me,' she said.

'Oh my dear, that would be impossible. I've been thinking of you non-stop ever since I left you on your birthday,'

'Well then come in.'

He stood hesitating in the hall. He noticed that the back door to the garden was shut, enclosing them in a resonant space with the rhythmic music of Prokofiev's *Romeo and Juliet*, the section known as *Dance of the Knights*.

'I wonder why you chose that Letty.'

'I hoped it might inflame you with its strong exciting beat.'

'I don't need any inflaming, my love.'

She laughed delightedly, and held out her arms to him. For a long moment they stood embracing as feelings of joy and relief, of desire and tenderness welded them together, till a sudden anxious thought made Ben stop kissing her hair.

'Is that crazy Crinkham woman snooping around?' he asked.

'No need to worry about her,' Letty reassured him. 'She's taken her binoculars to Hampton Court for the day.'

She took his hand and led him upstairs to her bedroom at the back of the house; they stood for a moment at the window with arms entwined round each other's waists to admire Letty's great rosebush below. He stroked her cheek, and kissed her neck, and undid the buttons of her shirt to reveal her firm round breasts. They were, he believed, the most beautiful things he'd ever seen.

'They're like the apples in the garden of Eden. So beautiful! No wonder Adam fell.' He thought: They are the key that unlocks all the secrets of the world.

But when he tried to loosen the belt of her trousers she checked him.

'You know I have a withered leg,' she said.

He silenced her objections with a long kiss. And when her trousers fell to the floor, and she stood naked, with shy, bent head, he knelt down, pressing his face against her shrivelled thigh, and kissed the little valley of her groin, murmuring: 'It only makes the rest of you more lovely.'

She felt then as if her heart had dropped out of her body, and thought: I could die for this man.

His best Sunday suit had never seemed a greater impediment to freedom as he began to undress, while Letty laughed at him from the bed:

'Oh do keep your tie on! I do love a naked man wearing a tie!'

They were too eager in their lovemaking that first time; they were like a canoe racing over a turbulent current, shooting the rapids and falling at last into a quiet pool beyond.

As they lay face to face, their arms round each other, exhausted by their struggle, he stroked her back and asked: 'How did it happen? Your leg, I mean?'

'Polio,' she replied briefly.

'I thought that disease was banished long ago by vaccination.'

'Should have been. Only my mother didn't believe in it – vaccination that is. She refused to let me have it. Believed vaccination interfered with Nature. 'Trust Nature' was her motto. She forgot that Nature, when left to her own devices, kills more young creatures than she saves. And I suppose Dad couldn't make up his mind to override her daft decision. I picked up the infection at a summer camp.'

He kissed her gently, imagining what she must have suffered, not only at the time of the illness, but afterwards, during her school years when, unable to take part in sports, standing always on the edge of playing-field and dance-floor, she could only watch others run and dance while she was forced to drag her disability under averted, or pitying, or even taunting eyes.

'My mother was a hippie, you see. She fell for all that hocus-pocus: flower-power, magic herbs, laying-on and linking of hands when not too busy rolling joints. I don't believe she was ever a junkie, though. Dad used to say she never went down the heroin path. After polio struck me they quarrelled furiously, he shouting, she throwing things, while I cowered under the kitchen table miserably, believing I was the cause of all the rows.'

He stroked her back gently, trying to soothe away her painful memories.

'In the end she left us. Walked out hand in hand with her witch-doctor lover, who must have comforted her, I suppose. Assuaged her guilt with hash no doubt. My Dad brought me up in the Mountside Music Academy; and after a time we stopped missing her. She just disappeared from our lives. They must have wandered round the world together, she and that Bogus Boy, because we got postcards from them occasionally from faraway exotic places. I don't know where they ended up. I suppose she's still alive somewhere.'

'Dear Letty,' he murmured. 'Darling girl! I wish I could help you to forget it all.'

'Oh no, Ben!' she protested. 'We are what we remember, I do believe. If we forget such things how can we make a better world?'

There was truth in that, he thought; but how could she ever be at peace with herself if she couldn't forgive her own mother, couldn't wash away the bitterness? It distressed him to think that the two people in her life who should have loved her most, her mother and the father of her son, had both betrayed her trust. He was overcome with tender reverence for her brave spirit. What she needed was love, healing, consoling love.

He found himself saying: 'What you need, Letty my darling, is love. And that's what I'm going to give you, lots and lots of it.'

3

The house was usually empty when Ben got home, but on this Sunday evening the emptiness gave him an uneasy feeling, as if he had lost something.

He went upstairs to his own bedroom, which had been the spare room before Celia moved him into it. He was used to sleeping alone; he had accepted all that eight years ago when Celia decided, and he'd agreed, that what with the mortgage, and running the car, even on their two salaries they couldn't afford more than two children, simply couldn't risk another pregnancy; and so she'd pushed him out of her bed. In any case she was determined to get back to work at the college where she'd been struggling to keep her job in-between coping with babies. She even had ambition enough to hope for a deputy headship one day. Of course he had agreed with her; but he couldn't help knowing that the arrangement suited her better than it did him. She had always rather disliked sex. At first she tried to hide her repugnance from him. Then there came a time when she began to adopt strategies to avoid it: turning her back on him in bed, twisting her mouth away from kisses, making the sort of excuses that were the common jokes of stand-up comics, sitting up half the night to watch the late movie on TV to make sure he was asleep before she climbed into the double bed, and finally pushing him out of it and into the celibate single in the spare room.

She allowed him to believe that her love was of a more refined and spiritual sort than his, letting him feel that he was pestering her, that his crude caresses bored her, gave her no peace with his uncomprehending male insensitivity to her moods. And as he lay awake in the long hours during those first few months of his exile he felt he was a failure, felt humiliated, unwanted and alone. He had bowed to her wishes, suppressing his anger and misery as best he could. But when she was converted to Catholicism, and explained that they couldn't have sex because it would be against the principles of her religion to use contraceptives, he did not suppress the comment that her new morality accorded remarkably well with her natural desires. She made no reply to that, simply turned away with pursed lips; and from that moment there was a clearly demarcated frontier between what they could and what they could not discuss. The silence that fell thickened with time, separating them more firmly, but also, in time, deadening the pain.

There had been days when his confidence in himself and his future failed utterly, leaving him with a taste of ashes in his mouth and a question on his tongue: Was life really worth all the effort he put into it? Only once had he wondered if a few gasps of carbon monoxide from the car's exhaust and an easeful death wouldn't be preferable. But then he thought of his children, how charming and loving they were, how much they still needed him; and in his mind's ear he heard the oboe playing the motif of the second movement of Brahms's Violin Concerto and felt again the joy of it. And he remembered his old man saying, that time he'd come blubbing home from school because some bully had teased him: 'Life isn't all joy-riding, you know. We have to put up with things'.

Which was what he'd been doing for the last eight years, putting up with things, letting his work and the small pleasures of existence fill his days. He and Celia were, after all, decent, well-intentioned people, so they continued to behave in a civilized manner, speaking kindly and politely to each other, sharing, wherever possible, domestic chores and caring for the children. What's more, real kindness and affection of a sort did persist between them.

Ben began to prepare the tea for his returning family. He laid the table in the kitchen, poured cornflakes into a bowl for Chris, hiding a few Smarties in among them as a surprise, cut thin slices of brown bread-and-butter, which his daughter liked to spread with jelly marmalade, and thought this was all more like breakfast than a tea-time meal, but it was what they wanted when they came home from Gran's. He heard the front door open as he put the kettle on.

Chris dropped his snorkel in the hall before rushing into the kitchen.

'I can swim a whole length under water!' he shouted, jumping into his father's arms.

Sarah walked through the back door to hang damp swimsuits on the washing-line.

'Hullo Dad!' she called over her shoulder. She was more orderly, and her approach to her father more sedate than her brother's.

In the doorway Celia stood, as usual overloaded with the weekend's paraphernalia: towels, pullovers, suntan lotion, sunglasses, books and paper tissues.

'Hullo dear!' she said. 'We're a bit late. Hope you weren't worried. Some hold-up on the motorway. Remains of an accident, I suppose.'

An image of Letty dead-heading her roses superimposed itself on his wife's presence, unnerving him, and again that feeling of emptiness invaded him as he thought: *I'm an outsider now in my own house. I don't really belong here any more.* He felt guilty, too, as he found himself looking at Celia as a stranger might. She was still a handsome woman, though she had grown heavier, moved more slowly, and had lost that vibrancy, that quick eagerness to share ideas and feelings that once she had. He remembered that when he first heard her name he'd imagined her as Cecilia, patron saint of musicians. But she was not musical at all. Well, you couldn't really blame her for that – could you? – any more than you could blame a woman for having brown instead of golden hair. Celia's hair had been blonde, and once so thick, abundant and beautiful that he always remembered the young Celia as the embodiment of Yeats's poem: *Never shall a young man / Thrown into despair / By those great honey-coloured / Ramparts at your ear / Love you for yourself alone/ And not your yellow hair.*

That was it, he supposed. He had loved her for her hair, and for the romance of her name, not knowing her self at all till the wear and tear of married life had torn away her disguises. Her hair was cropped short now, in keeping with the utilitarian image of brusque efficiency her feminist ideology dictated to her; and her eyes, once so bright and loving, now rested on him wearily.

'Beastly traffic,' he said. 'You must be dog-tired. Here, let me put all that stuff away. And come and sit down.'

Sighing gratefully she sat down at the table while he poured her a mug of tea. 'What a good sort you are, Ben,' she said.

No, he thought. She would never divorce him. Her religion didn't allow divorce. And was divorce what Letty wanted? In a sudden panic, fearing that Celia might read his thoughts in his face, he turned away, gave himself a moment to recover. Who had said anything about divorce anyway? It was far too soon to begin thinking along those lines, though he guessed Letty would want him, all of him, and would hate to share him with another woman. This unexpected glimpse of an unknown and possibly destructive future made his hands shake. But for crying out loud! he scolded himself. He was not an adolescent. He was a married man in a situation that thousands of men went through, that he himself had been through scores of times in imagination, though never before with such sharp anxiety. He reminded himself of Celia's many virtues: she was a really good person, altruistic, hard-working, devoted to the children of course, and actually seemed contented, without too much desire to keep up with the Bushbridge Joneses, so that their joint account didn't flush red too often.

He sat down at the table opposite Sarah.

'We went for quite a long walk in a wood,' said Celia.

'And we heard a woodpecker,' said Chris.

'But not the green kind in my book of common birds,' said Sarah. 'I saw him. He was black and white, with a bit of red, so I think he must have been an uncommon bird.'

'And he has a hammer in his beak. I heard him hammering,' Chris nodded solemnly. 'Two times.'

'Twice,' his sister corrected him. She was right. Sarah, like her mother, was usually right.

They finished the meal in silence, subdued by the relaxation following the activities of the day. When at last the children went upstairs, where they had a television of their own, and Ben was clearing the table, he said:

'They're good kids, Celia. Lovely really. We've been lucky, haven't we? Though perhaps I shouldn't say so, for fear of jealous gods, or the evil eye, or whatever . . . .'

Celia didn't fear the evil eye. She uttered a silent prayer to Jesus Lover of Little Children for their safety, and suffered no anxieties.

But ten minutes later there was a howl of rage from Chris, a squeal from Sarah, a thudding of angry feet overhead, and a video hurtled downstairs, ricocheting from banister to banister.

'What on earth is the matter?' demanded Ben, as he ran into the hall.

On the landing above Chris glowered, legs apart and fists at a pugilistic ready.

'I want Star Wars!' he bellowed. 'Not girls' crap about a secret garden!'

On Monday afternoons Ben gave private piano lessons in the sitting-room. The other front room, formerly a dingy dining-room, had been converted into a leisure space for Celia. They never gave dinner parties like some of their neighbours; the occasional guest ate with them in the kitchen. Most of Ben's room was occupied by his grand piano, which he was playing when his first pupil arrived. She stood in the doorway listening as he played one of the pieces set for her LUMCA examination in a fortnight's time.

'Hullo Alison,' he greeted her. This twelve-year-old was one of his best pupils. She had some talent, a good ear, and actually cared about the music.

She sat down on the piano-stool and began to play the first section of Schubert's Piano Sonata in A minor, while he encouraged her, humming the melody.

'You must make your fingers sing,' he told her. 'That's what Chopin said: "Sing with your fingers!" ' And when she finished her set piece he praised her. 'It's coming along nicely. You'll do it well in the exam. So don't worry. Practise it every day, but not for too long, or you'll get bored with it; and then it'll sound mechanical. Now let's have the next piece.'

She turned the page of her music book. She knew the next piece was more difficult; but she began to attack it *con spirito*, as directed by its composer, Schumann. Mr Fording said the funny title, *Grillen*, meant whims or caprices, but she thought of it as hot spitting bits of fat on her dad's barbecue, when they were all having fun in the garden, and laughing at Dad in his cook's apron.

'That's good,' he said. 'Now what about some scales and arpeggios? We should have had them first really, shouldn't we? An easy one to start with. Let's try F major before we dash into E flat minor.'

She made a face at the mention of E flat minor; but then she met his grin, which made her laugh. She liked Mr Fording; she even liked playing maddening scales for him.

For Ben the day was passing, pushing Letty's image away from the forefront of his attention. He knew she was at work, so he couldn't ring her, even had it been prudent to do so. No. He'd have to wait till Sunday to see her, even to hear her voice.

Till then he could only hold her in memory and imagination. The week was going to pass slowly for him, but he knew he must resign himself to waiting. Patience was something life had taught him.

Letty waited inside St Augustine's for Ben to finish his dismissal music, enjoying the reverberation of chords in the rafters and the calm atmosphere inside the church which was wonderfully cool on this hot July Sunday. Ben was not going to jog across the common; he was going to walk with her through what the older residents of the place called 'the village' on their way to lunch at Toni's. When the church was almost empty of worshippers Ben descended from his organ loft and joined her in the nave. He took her arm, and together they went out through the shadowed stone porch into the brutal-bright light and heat of noon.

'You look sad,' Letty said.

'Just thinking.'

'And thinking makes you sad?' She noticed how quiet the place was, how free of traffic compared with its Monday bustle, as they walked up the High Street, past Colman's, *Grocer to the Gentry. Established 1860*, where in the old days she used to buy her father's favourite Gentleman's Relish to spread on his toast for tea. Colman's probably still sold it along with coffee beans, non-bagged teas from Darjeeling and Assam, crystallized ginger from China, Bath Oliver biscuits, good olive-oil, Parmesan cheese and other not yet commercially processed foods; but it was too expensive for her to shop there nowadays, except perhaps at Christmas if she wanted to buy someone an extravagant gift.

They walked towards the Common, to Prince's Pond, where they stopped to watch some boys playing with model yachts. What might have been charmingly idyllic was spoiled by heaps of rubbish scattered along the path.

'Good God! Do you see that?' exclaimed Ben as they sat down on a bench in the shade of a hawthorn tree. A boy of about ten, wearing a green T-shirt with the letters G.E.S. emblazoned on its chest, was picking up all the litter (plastic bags, empty soft-drinks cans and cigarette packets) and dropping it into the bins provided by the local council but seldom used.

'I expect he's a member of this new group, the Green Earth Savers,' said Letty. 'It's a new charity but some of the schools are hooking on to it. But why are you sad?'

'I want to be with you all the time, my lovely, not only on Sundays. I suppose that's greedy of me?'

'And you can't be, because of course you're married. Tangled up and tied down. I might have guessed.' Her voice was harsh. He told her then that he had two children and a wife, Celia, whom he'd once worshipped.

'We sleep in separate rooms,' he said; and when Letty looked startled he tried to explain: 'Oh, it's all right. I'm used to it now. It's been going on for eight years.'

'But that's terrible! You're not a monk. It's not a marriage at all, is it?'

Ben immediately wanted to protect his wife from Letty's indignation. 'Celia's a good sort, you know. A very nice person. Everybody likes her. It's just that she doesn't like sex.'

'But that's not normal Ben. Why haven't you been to some therapist about it?' She sounded angry.

'Oh, I don't know. I suppose I believe we're not all made the same way. I don't think there's much you can do about it if your partner no longer attracts you. I just don't turn her on, you see.'

She put her arms round, him and murmured: 'Oh, my poor darling!' Thinking: *Eight years in a stony wilderness* . . . . She asked: 'Surely you haven't been faithful to her all that time?'

'I've flirted with a pretty smile sometimes. And occasionally I've fancied a nice bum, although I've never gone in for bottom-pinching, so much frowned on in London.'

'Isn't it everywhere?'

'Toni tells me that in Italy it's a humanitarian gesture.' When she laughed he added: 'I've never been in love like this before.'

Toni noticed their sad solemn faces when they entered the restaurant, and knew they must have been having serious talk. Toni didn't like serious talk, which was absolutely inimical to the proper enjoyment of good cooking. Assuming his most electric smile he led them to the table by the window where, with a ritual flourish of his snowy napkin to dispel melancholy, he assured them of the most beautiful food to come.

'Today I give you for a starter something new. Not Italian. It is Turkish aubergine. Was made, once upon a time, for Muslim imam. Was so good in the smell department, from so many 'erbs and oils, that this priest, he faint away from 'appiness.' He was pretty sure it would make Mr Fording and his lady happy, though he hoped they wouldn't faint away.

It was indeed delicious. It was after the second glass of Pinot Grigio, and when they were finishing Toni's special *ossobuco* with saffron rice sprinkled with aromatic herbs, that Ben told her he had to spend a week in Athens in October, examining aspiring young musicians for LUMCA.

'It'll be quite hot still,' he said. 'I suppose it wouldn't be possible for you to take your summer holiday then and come with me? We might go to Crete for a few days afterwards, and swim in the Aegean.'

'Oh Ben!' she gasped. 'How marvellous that would be!' She began to think about the possibility of exchanging holiday dates with someone else in the office. It would be difficult with so little time in which to arrange the swap, but, who knew? There might be someone willing.

'I'll see what I can do,' she said. 'We might be lucky.'

Jude was surprised, when he let himself in, to find the house empty. He'd rung earlier to announce his coming, but the phone had not been answered. Letty was usually at home on Sunday morning, so he wondered where she could be. Her absence was annoying. He wanted to see her before he left for Angola, but he didn't have much time, as his sudden leave of absence was very brief. He went straight up to his bedroom to pack a few belongings he wanted to take with him, and then went down into the kitchen to cook himself a snack. He was even more surprised, then, to come face to face with a small boy who was helping himself to a slice of apple pie from the fridge.

'How did you get here?' he asked.

Without a word the child led him into the front sitting-room, and pointed at the window. 'She left it open, didn't she?' he explained. 'I never nicked nuffing.' He added when they got back to the kitchen: 'Never 'ad no breakfast, see?' Jude assumed he was one of the waifs and strays Letty occasionally picked up and pampered, and very soon he was cooking scrambled eggs on toast for the two of them. As the child ate he stared at the front page of Letty's Sunday paper spread out on the table before him.

'What's this then?' he asked, his forefinger touching a photo of a man in a white coat with his hand on the back of a sheep.

'You can read, can't you?' from Jude.

'Not much.' He spelled out slowly: 'D – O – L – L– Y. Who's Dolly?'

Jude groaned softly. He could see himself getting into all sorts of trouble trying to explain genetic cloning, a subject which he himself found obscure, and which no doubt would be nothing but black magic to this illiterate child. He was relieved when he heard the turning of a key in a lock, and Isadora Crinkham came into the room, all her scarves floating out behind her with the flurry of her entry. She stood still when she saw them.

'Quite a party!' she said. 'And who's this?'

'I don't know,' replied Jude, his mouth full. 'He came in through a window at the front. It seems Letty left it open.'

'A good thing for you you didn't try the back way, or I'd have caught you in my binoculars,' said Isadora. The boy was staring at her as if she was some strange exotic animal. 'He must be a little prole from beyond the alley,' she said. 'I wonder if Letty knows him?'

'What's she on about?' the child spoke sharply. 'I'm a Brit, not a Paki nor nuffing. And the lady wot lives 'ere, she said I could 'elp meself from the fridge. I never nicked nuffing!'

'Food being not nuffing but stuffing, I suppose.'

There was a short silence. Jude didn't offer Isadora a seat. Then the boy said: 'She's talkin' crap. I said I never fuckin' nicked nuffing.'

In the lengthening silence Isadora gathered her scarves about her. 'We must protect the well of English undefiled. Too many meaningless craps and fucks will certainly pollute the water.'

'The well of English won't mean much to him,' said Jude. 'He can't read.'

'I can read this,' said the boy, pointing at Dolly's photo, but Isadora could see that Jude's comment had needled him and made him feel ashamed.

'Where's Mum?' asked Jude.

'She's gone out to lunch with her fancy-man.'

It was Jude's turn to look needled and ashamed, though he tried to suppress these feelings, which he knew sprang chiefly from primitive emotions some people blamed on Oedipus. Still, her absence was annoying when he wanted to see her, might not see her again for months. Last time he saw her, about seven weeks ago, she certainly had no lover hanging about the place. Where had this new man sprung from?

'I'm leaving the country tomorrow,' he said. 'I don't know for how long. Africa. I shall have to write her a note.'

'Africa?' echoed the boy.

'Yes.'

'Will it be dangerous then?'

'It will – rather.'

'Cor!' breathed the little prole.

4

Neither Barney nor Isadora were pleased with the changes going on at Number 11. Letty explained to them with due consideration for their feelings and interests, and very reasonably, that since Sunday was the only day she and Ben could spend together she must give that time to him. That meant that the Sunday lunches she had been cooking for her two neighbours would henceforward be served on Saturdays. Isadora knew she had to accept the new order of things, but she didn't do it with a good grace. It would entirely upset her weekend. For one thing she'd have to curtail her delightfully leisurely combing through the stalls at the Saturday antiques market up on the Mount, for another she'd have to spend a tediously long and boring Sunday at home by herself, with nothing to entertain her till the evening, when she could switch on the telly for the Antiques Roadshow. She was being kicked out into this dull Sunday alone, but worse than that she was being demoted; Letty was pushing her out of her place as significant friend and green planet partner for a newcomer who hadn't much to say for himself and in her opinion very little to recommend him. He was of course a man, still relatively young, all his limbs and features as far as she could judge, were still intact, and, she remembered, he had his own teeth, while her new dentures were giving her one hell of discomfort and embarrassment. She could only suppose Letty was still of an age when she was susceptible to males, perhaps even felt the need of one. Women were so silly over men, as she herself, she had to admit, had been in the past. She just hoped, devoutly, that Letty's little love scamper would not develop into a scenario too dreadful to contemplate, but which she nevertheless contemplated: Letty falling seriously in love, Letty getting married and going to live elsewhere. And then the inevitable break-up of this wonderful, special relationship of three they had all shared for the last five or six years, a partnership for their mutual benefit, as it had proved to be, but also an experiment in a better-for-the-planet, a greener sort of living, a happier, more environmentally friendly existence than people all around them knew how to enjoy. Well, Letty won't get rid of me too easily, she promised herself grimly. ' "I am a kind of burr, and I shall stick." ' She spoke aloud, but softly, repeating the words of the Bard till they acquired the potency of a mantra.

Barney too, as he watered the tomatoes in his greenhouse, was thinking about Letty and Ben. Were they seriously in love? And if so what might this new situation do to the special form of family life for single people that was being evolved at Nos. 10, 11 and 12 Alexandra Terrace?

Through the blurred wet glass he watched Isadora tottering along the path. He knew what she'd been up to, poking her nose into things that shouldn't concern her. But of course they *did* concern her, and him as well. You couldn't live in any sort of family without getting tangled up in the private affairs of its members.

'You shouldn't wear those high heels,' he told her, as she put her head inside the greenhouse door.

'My word! It's hot in here!' she gasped, fanning herself with the loose end of a scarf.

'They make you totter,' he pursued relentlessly. 'And one day you'll slip and fall, and break your femur. And that will be the end of you.'

'Not at all!' she argued airily. 'Nowadays they put a pin inside to make the bits of bone join up. That's what happened to Mrs Blum at Number 6. She was out of hospital in the twinkling of an eye. And *she* has osteoporosis, poor thing! So her bones are extra fragile, which mine are *not*.'

He nodded. He knew what she'd come to talk about, and it wasn't osteoporosis.

'Been spying on the lovebirds, have you?' he asked, turning away from her to pinch out some unwanted shoots from his tomato plants. He adopted towards Isadora, as towards most people he met, a slightly contemptuous banter. Barney didn't think much of the human race. He had seen too much of the ugly side of its Janus mask. His father, now long dead, had been London Irish, a family man who loved his wife but suffered from a weakness endemic in his native land, the tendency to take a drop too much too often, and when drunk he was violent. He never hit his wife, because she remained silent when all the suppressed rage and disappointments of his life erupted into colourful and abusive rhetoric, but his children, irritated by his jibes, and less patient than their mother, often argued with him. And then they were punched, and if they fell, kicked. It was inevitable that as they grew up they all left home, one by one, emigrated all over the globe, one son to Australia, another to Canada, and two daughters to the USA. Barney, who was the youngest, was sixteen when war was declared. He saw this as an opportunity to escape from home, and falsifying his age by two years managed to enlist with the British army as part of the poor bloody infantry.

During the débâcle of Dunkirk he found himself being herded along with a group of 'other ranks', but without an officer, into a German cattle-truck bound on a long, long, uncomfortable and thirsty journey East. Afterwards he was moved about from POW camp to POW camp, made to work for the enemy on all sorts of agricultural and reconstruction projects, endured things, and saw worse things that he didn't want to remember, but which sometimes, even now, after more than half a century, broke through his dreams, waking him, making him cry out in the small hours of darkness between one day and the next, when nobody could hear him, except his own Mavis, lying quietly asleep beside him. He went into the war a strong and cheerful boy, and often thanked his strength and cheerfulness, as well as the gift of being able to hold his tongue, which he'd inherited from his mother, for the way he survived; he came out of it a man, silent and embittered, disliking the male section of the human race. He preferred women, whom he regarded as the better half of humanity, and had loved his wife, whom he still missed greatly. He believed in love, in its redemptive power, and the way it could transform, even if only briefly, ordinary none too saintly people.

So his attitude to this affair of Letty and Ben was not the same as Isadora's. Letty he loved, less with lust than with a kind of wistful reverence. If Ben made her happy, well good luck to them! That he might remove her from their commune didn't bear thinking about; but it might never come to that, so he refused to think about it. Instead he concentrated on the present. Ben seemed to him a decent sort of chap, a church organist and teacher of music, wasn't he? That sort of person should be incapable of unkindness, so perhaps Letty would be safe. Then he thought of Germany, and all the musical geniuses Germany had produced, and suddenly an image came back to him of a Saturday afternoon during the war. He was being held in one of the camps for British prisoners of war scattered about Silesia. A German guard took him, along with two other Brits, to do some work putting up shelves in the sergeants' mess at a German army barracks near a village, whose name he never discovered. It was difficult to know exactly where he was because the POWs were continually moved from camp to camp, no doubt in order to prevent their becoming too familiar with their surroundings, which might have aided escape. When the work was done they were marched back to their own camp, but on the way the guard stopped at the village.

Some sort of festival is taking place on the green, around which are trees, and under them tables where soldiers sit drinking beer, laughing and joking. The atmosphere is relaxed and jolly as the guard halts his group of POWs in order to exchange pleasantries with some of the soldiers, and is offered a jar of beer. A man wearing an apron goes from table to table refilling glasses and tankards, and a fat woman with red cheeks, who may be his wife, follows him with a dish of sausages. Barney's mouth waters as he smells the spiced meat. He is always hungry, and he longs for one of those sausages with a passionate longing. One of the German soldiers, who is certainly a bit tipsy, seeing the three Brits standing there in silence, suddenly hands his own glass to Barney, commanding him to drink and give his mates a share. It's a warm afternoon in June, and the trees must be lime trees, because the scent of their flowers overpower, even the smell of beer. He notices, while sipping it with relish, that on some of the tables people are standing. One is a young Polish woman, quite pretty, too, he thinks. Round her neck is a noose of rope, and from it is suspended a placard printed with words in German, which even he can translate: *Sie sagte Nein*. The guard catches Barney's eye, and laughs, saying: 'She won't say No again. Eh?' And Barney, not yet fully understanding, returns a subservient smile, the memory of which will make him squirm with remorse for ever afterwards. On another table stands a bearded Polish peasant, his eyes closed and his chin sunk over his placard, which proclaims that he has denied milk to German soldiers. Barney sees that the rope round his neck has been thrown over a branch above and knotted. As Barney's mouth falls open, the froth from his beer still on his lips, there is a sudden shout, and all the soldiers begin drumming their knuckles on the tables. A shot is fired, and immediately they rise and begin to sing as they drag the tables away from the trees. That girl who has resisted rape, pawing the air like a dog scrambling at a door as she dangles, still haunts his dreams; but he can't remember what song they sang.

The German genius for music had not curbed the Nazi appetite for cruelty, he reflected. And Hitler himself was said to have been devoted to Wagnerian opera.

Ben, of course, thank heavens, was English; and Barney
trusted to his own gut feeling about him, that he would be
good to Letty, whom Barney loved as the daughter he and
Mavis never had. Mavis would have loved her too, if she'd
known her; but it wasn't till after Mavis died that Letty bought
the house next door. Their friendship began over the fence that
then divided their gardens. It was during a conversation about
compost, and how worms converted vegetable waste into
good soil, that he discovered that Letty was the right sort.
When she spoke of compost as 'a lovely, soft, rich tilth' his
heart warmed to her. She talked about feeding plants as if she
really cared about them; and he guessed then that she was a
person who wouldn't hurt others. Her voice was gentle, but
her hands holding the top of the intervening fence were
strong. She had a worker's hands, and he knew at once that
she was made of the right stuff. It was only later that he saw
her walking, saw her limp, and learned about her childhood
infection with poliomyelitis; and the pity he felt turned his
liking into love.

'So don't interfere,' he told Isadora. 'Keep out of it. Let them
be happy.'

'How can they be happy, Barney, if the man's already
married?' she objected.

'There are different degrees of marriage,' he said. 'And you
know they're going away to Greece for ten days? That should be
long enough to test them.'

'I do believe he's going to break her heart.'

'Let's wait and see, shall we? *Che sera sera*.' He was pleased to
see by her expression that for once she could call to mind no apt
quotation to confound his little Italian phrase. He had scored a

point. 'You can take your tomatoes,' he said, nodding towards a punnet filled with her favourite cherry tomatoes. 'And there's a couple of Little Gems ready for you too.' He emerged from the greenhouse to pull the lettuces out of the ground, and shook their roots free of earth.

'Thank you, Barney,' she said meekly. Carrying her booty she crossed the bottom of Letty's garden and walked up to her own, pausing for a moment to examine her damson tree and note that the fruit was ripening, before making her way to the bow window in her sitting-room, where she sat, surveying, through her binoculars, the full extent of Prole Alley to where the old right-of-way opened out into Chaplin Walk with its shoddy post-war housing.

Isadora had been silenced, but she was far from defeated. Of course she loved Letty, just as much as Barney did, and more, since she had made up her mind to stick to her. She had always planned to spend her final, her sick and helpless days, at home; but who would look after her then? Her only relative, her niece, would not. Why should she? She lived too far away, and loved her aunt too little to be able to undertake such a job. But Letty would look after her, or at least would oversee the home helps and hired nurses who would undoubtedly be necessary at the end. So the thought of Letty's leaving Alexandra Terrace to set up house with Ben filled her with anxiety; and rising panic made her heart beat wildly as she contemplated the nursing home for the aged: the other inmates all more gaga than herself, the bossy nurses putting her firmly in her dependent place, calling her by her Christian name when they were not acquainted, knew nothing of her, her past, and what she'd done, whose souls, like the sausages and meat pies they fed on, were gross, without one will-o'-the-wisp of wit, certainly no understanding of poetry, and who, if they had heard of Shakespeare, probably would regard him as a boring old fart, because they lacked the concentration and the politeness to listen to his lines. They might know how to clean out commodes, but when it came to the well of English undefiled, and the glories of our language, they wouldn't recognize arse from elbow, poor ignorant cows! In such a place the food would be virtually uneatable, consisting of overcooked vegetables and stews on which floating fat congealed. Real coffee would not be brewed, and tea would be a cup of scalding water poured over the dusty dregs of leaves spurned by the Indian peasants who had picked them. She could foresee vividly how she would descend into a Dante's Inferno before she had even passed through the portals of the grave. And it was Letty alone who could prevent all this from happening.

Isadora sat for a long time, thinking.

On Saturday, when Letty was safely out of the way, flying happily to Athens with Ben, holding hands with him in the plane as it took off, blissfully willing to die together should they crash . . . . Isadora imagined the scene as she unlocked the backdoor of Number 11 and went into the house. No music boomed in the hall, and the unusual silence seemed to her uncanny. She felt a little shiver run down her spine as she climbed the stairs and entered Letty's bedroom. She couldn't bear to look at the bed, now tidily covered with a white quilt, but once the cradle for all passion spent. Instead she examined the bedside table, hoping to find an address book by the phone. In this she was disappointed, but there were two crumpled letters, which she picked up and read. They were both from Ben, ordinary vulgar little reassurances of undying love, was how she judged them. They were undated, and had no address; but one was still in its envelope, with a legible postmark: Bushbridge. So that was where the real Mrs Fording lived. It was enough to be going on with. She smiled as she carefully replaced the letters.

A voice, Barney's voice, startled her as she was about to leave the room.

'Is there anyone up there?' he called from the back door, guessing it was Isadora poking her nose into other folks' private affairs.

She came downstairs swinging a bunch of keys.

'Letty asked me to come in every day, you know, to make sure everything was all right – pull curtains, turn on lights, that sort of thing, to give outsiders the impression that the house is not unoccupied.'

'OK,' he said grudgingly. 'But she asked me to check all the windows and doors were locked at night.'

'Yes, of course,' agreed Isadora airily. 'Your eyes to keep watch on the outside of the house, mine to guard the inside . . . we should be able to keep it safe from intruders, shouldn't we?' She smiled archly.

He watched her face closely as she came level with him. What's the scheming old bitch up to? he wondered.

'I'm off now to the Antiques Market,' she said. 'I'll be there all afternoon.' She would take the bus up to the Mount and walk back downhill. She could still manage that. She was beaming happily at the prospect of browsing through heaps of Victorian curios and ephemera, her eyes positively glittering with the anticipation of feeling all that decaying rubbish. Well, good luck to her! He just hoped she hadn't pinched something belonging to Letty to sell to one of those harpies in the market.

Isadora, leafing through the telephone directory, found there were a great many Fords but only a handful of Fordings listed, of whom two lived in Bushbridge. One had initials G.W., but immediately above him was B.S. That must be Benjamin's number, she thought as she dialled it, wondering what S stood for. She was tense and excited, and her mind, like an eager puppy, raced all over the place, sniffing at trifles. Could it be Sebastian, shot full of arrows like the saint? S might, of course, stand for a surname. Sebastian had been her former husband's name. She remembered him in a disastrous performance of *Hamlet* in York. Or was it Harrogate? He played Fortinbras in a black leather jacket and high black boots, looking every inch the Hell's Angel rather than the noble soldier. He was a small man, and his sword was too long for him. He tripped over it as he crossed the hall at Elsinore and fell with a crash among the Danish royal corpses. His helmet came off and tumbled towards the footlights. She had felt no sympathy for him in his humiliation, so great had been her own.

The audience didn't object to this version of the play, but laughed and clapped, shouting: *Encore! Encore!* She could see his toothbrush moustache now. Like Hitler's. It was on that disastrous tour that she mislaid Crinkham, (poor wretched Sebastian!). He was needed for the part of Polonius, which suited him better than the unfortunate Fortinbras, and sometimes for Bottom in *A Midsummer Night's Dream*. It was all a tale best untold, properly unremembered.

'Celia Fording speaking.'

'Oh! Yes . . . Mrs Fording? I'm ringing on behalf of the tourist agency. It's about the double room in Athens for next week. I understand you wanted to cancel the single?' She waited for a perceptible pause before continuing: 'The hotel Apollo can let you have a double with a balcony looking towards the Acropolis.' She paused to take a breath. 'There will, of course, be a small extra charge for the room with a view . . . Is that agreeable to you?' Her voice rose to a question mark.

'I'm afraid there must be some mistake,' said Mrs Fording from Bushbridge. 'My husband's already in Athens. He left yesterday.'

Isadora waited for the shock of this information to sink in before apologizing: 'Oh! I'm so sorry! I seem . . .' she stumbled, 'I seem to have confused the bookings. So sorry to have troubled you!' she trilled, and hung up, congratulating herself that she was still able to bring it off, that even after years of unemployment her thespian skills had not deserted her.

Celia wondered what all that was about as she replaced the receiver. What an affected voice the woman had! – almost as if she were acting a part. Some computer muddle, I suppose, she told herself. It was only later that she remembered that the woman had given no name for the tourist agency. She felt a dart of suspicion that the caller had been trying to discover if the house was empty during Ben's absence abroad. Well, it wasn't; and she hoped that her voice and her presence would scare away any possible burglar. She did not connect that phone conversation with the parcel she received, a few mornings later, addressed to her in handwriting scrawled with a black felt pen. She unwound the tissue-paper-wrapped object carefully, then dropped it with a sudden squawk. It was some sort of corkscrew, probably Victorian, or perhaps Edwardian, an antique really, she thought, as she picked it up from the floor, a piece of old fashioned pornography in the shape of a pair of female legs, button-booted and attached by the thigh joints to the screw, on which someone had left a cork. Celia could see that as the cork ascended the legs would part. She noticed, too, that one of the thigh joints was damaged, so the whole thing seemed unstable and rather fragile.

Who could have sent her this? And why? There was no letter, no explanation of any sort. Could it be somebody's dirty joke? She thought of other college teachers, of her friends, of Ben's friends, and even some of his pupils. It was the sort of thing a naughty boy might do for a dare. Could it be that teenage lad who came for piano lessons on Friday evenings? A big boy, certainly sexually mature. She made a wry face, remembering his adolescent acne and his harsh, breaking voice. There had been times when she'd wondered . . . The way he hung about in the hall, when he should have been eager to go, taking a long time to put on his anorak, searching for his baseball cap before leaving . . . hoping perhaps to see her, even exchange a word or two . . . And once he had ventured into her sanctum, without knocking, to ask for a glass of water. She began to wonder, now, if the poor boy was having fantasies about her; but this . . . ! This was horrible! She would show it to Ben when he returned from Athens, and ask him what he made of it. In the meantime she had work to do, and couldn't waste any more precious minutes thinking about it.

'Hurry up, troops!' she called from the hall. 'We're late already!' She hustled the children out of the house and into the car, and checked their seat belts before driving off to begin her normal weekday routine: drop the kids at their school, drive to college, two morning lectures there before canteen lunch, French conversation and pronunciation class in the afternoon, handing back to students their exercises with comments and corrections, ten minutes for a cup of tea, pick up kids again, home to get their tea, brief interval while they watched some suitable telly, and she cleared up in the kitchen before they sat down in her sanctum to do homework and she to correct more of her students' exercises. After chasing Chris upstairs for his bath, and a little later shouting at him to hurry up and come down, Ben usually read to them both, Sarah always wanting to begin something new, while Chris held aggressively to a famil-iar story. *Charlie and the Chocolate Factory* was his favourite.

'It's the bookerest book, so there!' he declared to Sarah if she groaned because she had to listen to it yet again. Then at last there was a blessed hour, perhaps two, if Celia was lucky, when she could enjoy her own television, a radio talk, or read to herself in bed. She didn't have much time for talking with Ben, and very little for thinking either, still less for idle speculation. She often fell asleep at night with the light on, and her book in her hands. Then she slept the sleep of the truly tired, deeply, thankfully; but she did wake sometimes in the early hours to the terror of her own peculiar dream landscape: she was driving two horses downhill on a narrow lane strewn with boulders, and the cart she sat in swayed on rickety wheels. It was going faster and faster, and she couldn't see the end of the road because fog obliterated it, faster and faster and she could-n't stop. Sometimes she cried out at waking; then she thought of Ben sleeping in the next room, and wondered if her shout had woken him, but it never did. If he'd come in to comfort her, she thought, she would allow him into her bed; but she wouldn't allow herself to go to him. It would, of course, be utterly selfish to wake him.

5

Letty watched the other tourists tumble out of the Sounion bus, all chattering in their different languages as they followed their guides: German, Japanese, and a Frenchman in charge of a group of schoolchildren. They surged over the promontory on which the temple of Poseidon stood, while she followed at a more leisurely pace. She didn't immediately go to the temple but walked instead to the edge of the cliff and peered down at waves breaking on the rocks below. It was here, according to her guidebook, that Aegeus waited for the return of his son Theseus from Crete. It was on this spot, and it thrilled her to think she was standing on it, several thousand years later, that the anxious father waited to see the white sail signalling his son's triumphant homecoming. Theseus had undertaken the unenviable task of transporting seven young men and seven maidens from Attica to Crete as tribute to King Minos, who needed them to feed to the Minotaur. It was a human sacrifice made annually to the monster hidden in the labyrinth below his palace. Aegeus, as he waited, had no means of knowing that Theseus had killed the monster, had found his way out of the maze, had fallen in love with Ariadne, the king's daughter, eloped with her, and was now on his way home. Aegeus looked for the white sail, gazing out over Homer's wine-dark sea that now lay at Letty's feet, a calm unblinking mirror to the sky. She, too, gazed at it, thinking of all the islands scattered across it, remembering Byron:

The isles of Greece! The isles of Greece!
Where burning Sappho loved and sung,
Where grew the arts of war and peace,
Where Delos rose and Phoebus sprung!
Eternal summer gilds them yet,
But all, except their sun, is set.

Unfortunately Theseus forgot about the sail. Perhaps he was carousing too happily with his sailors; perhaps he fell asleep on watch. Whatever the reason, the old black sail remained at the mast as his ship approached Attica. Aegeus, standing on Sounion, saw it, and thinking his son's enterprise had failed, and that Theseus was dead, hurled himself off the cliff-top into the sea, ever afterwards called the Aegean.

Letty was leaning over, shivering a little as she tried to measure the distance of his fall, when a man, bearded and agitated, ran towards her. She guessed he must be a coastguard of sorts because he was shouting a warning in all the languages he could muster: 'Achtung! Arrêtez! Pericoloso! Stop!' She couldn't help laughing a little as she tried to explain in English that she was not suicidal, but was reliving an ancient Greek myth. He didn't understand her, but he calmed down when he caught the names of Theseus and Aegeus. He refused to leave her side, however, till she moved away from the cliff's edge to join the crowd among the pillars.

Somewhere here, she knew, on one of these, Byron had cut his name into the stone; and at last she found it crammed between two pieces of masonry. The column had obviously once been smashed, and fairly recently reconstructed to its present condition.

She wondered at what stage of his own odyssey Byron had visited Sounion. She often thought of Byron as a sort of brother because he was lame like her. She imagined him lying sick in Missolonghi as he waited for arms and cash from England to aid the Greeks in their fight for independence from the Turks, and receiving instead a load of English bibles to distribute among the freedom fighters, most of whom couldn't read their own, let alone a foreign language. Poor Byron! The shots he fired were all in print in his own personal war of independence for Greece, where he died. But not unsung. More biographies have been written about him, she believed, than any other man, except perhaps Napoleon.

It was very hot, and Letty sweated under her thin summer shirt as the bus re-entered the thick polluted air of afternoon in Athens. It's eternal summer here all right, she thought, although in England it must be cool by now, the autumn sun low, the slanting shadows long. Here the brazen sun forced its way down to the streets even through the pall of smog. She was glad to get back to the hotel, where she could take a cool shower, and lie down to rest a little before Ben returned from the hall near the university, where the examinations were being held, from all the sounds of girls and boys scraping fiddles, piping flutes, and stumbling through wrong notes on the piano.

'A Bach partita on the cello, if you please!' he'd exclaimed to her at breakfast that morning. A boy of twelve had tried to play it for him the day before. 'Gymnastics on strings!' was how he'd described it. 'Far too exacting for a child of twelve!'

The examinees were mostly the children of diplomats, or of expatriate businessmen living in Greece.

'Were they any good?' she'd asked.

'Average,' he'd replied. 'But there was one little Greek boy of no more than seven who played the flute as easily as he breathed.'

'A second James Galway with a golden flute?'

'No golden flute. Perhaps one day a celebrated flautist though. Who knows?'

Their hotel was small and unpretentious, but the restaurant was on the top floor, with windows open at night to let in the cooling air. As the day left the city so did the traffic with its insistent noises; and it was pleasant then to sit at their table by the window and look out over rooftops towards the Acropolis, to see the floodlit Parthenon in all its stark white splendour against the surrounding darkness, in an ambience impossible to achieve by day when it became a tower of Babel with thousands of tourists tramping round it, shaking the foundations of the sacred ruin. That tramping, Letty believed, did more harm than all the onslaughts time had thrown at it: the battering by war and weather, its use as a Florentine palace, a Turkish brothel, and when Elgin saw it, a camp for Turkish soldiers whose boots trod upon the famous frieze that had fallen to the ground and lay smashed into segments. Some pieces had been dragged away from the site and used as hearthstones, their carved reliefs blackened and eroded by camp fires, till Elgin rescued them.

'Somehow,' said Letty, 'in spite of all the insults history has hurled at it the Parthenon still stands in beauty unadorned.'

'The most perfect poem in stone, some French poet has called it,' said Ben. 'So I was told today by a French diplomat's son.'

As they sipped resin-flavoured wine and stared silently out towards the temple on the hill it was possible then to feel something of the miracle, to get an inkling of the glory that had been Greece in the time of Pericles, when Athenian power and wealth, and all her arts of war and peace had attained their apogee.

They didn't talk much; there was no need. Their fingers touched as they clinked glasses and exchanged soft glances.

'To Greece!' murmured Letty.

'To us!' said Ben.

They had made a tacit agreement that this ten days was to be an oasis in their lives, a green space in time for rest and joy, a jewel set in the gold of Byron's eternal summer. They were not going to think about the future and all the moral and emotional dilemmas in which they were trapped, and all the mundane difficulties that lay in wait, ready to smudge and smear this bright love of theirs. For this sweet interlude they were going to live entirely in the present.

At night when they made love quietly and tenderly, and afterwards when, free of thought, they lay suspended within the safe circle of each other's arms, they believed themselves to be in paradise. When they looked long and searchingly into each other's faces Ben could hear angelic voices, such as must rise in harmony around the throne of God, and Letty could discern, as she stroked the contours of his forehead, cheeks and chin the flower never hybridized, as yet unimagined, of the perfect rose. And when in the morning, after a breakfast of coffee with rolls and honey, before Ben strode out into the streets, choked with traffic and all the bustle of human lives, to begin his own day's work, he touched her cheek softly, wishing her another wonderful day, then Letty, smiling, thought of Louis Armstrong, and remembered his great, black, warm-hearted voice growling out in gratitude: *What a wonderful world!*

Humming his song she picked up her map of Athens and caught a bus to Omonia Square, and thence to the Archeological Museum, there to browse inside its cool, air-conditioned interior. The famous nude Aphrodite, about to smack Pan with her sandal for sexually harassing her, was a must; but after that she passed other statues of Venus and Poseidon rather quickly, bestowing only a passing glance on the bronze bareback jockey that had been salvaged from the sea. She was eager to get to the Mycenean room. When at last she saw the gold dug up at Mycenae by the famous German archeologist Heinrich Schliemann, and gazed at the gold death-mask, she couldn't help laughing a little, being tossed between delight and disbelief. It was a portrait of the universal soldier, the features as modern as they were classical, sharp-nosed, ascetic; the face might have been that of an English brigadier. But Schliemann, standing in that ancient grave, and carried away by the excitement of his discovery, had sent a telegram to the king of Greece: *I have looked on the face of Agamemnon.* Perhaps it was, for after the fall of Troy he returned to Mycenae, his homeland, to be murdered by his wife. Letty, seeing the mask behind the glass in the museum, could sense something of what Schliemann must have felt.

She carried her own excitement outside to the café in a quiet garden spread before the museum, and there sat down with a cup of coffee. She didn't in the least mind being alone in Athens. People in the streets and cafés all seemed serious and courteous; she was never jostled or harassed, and solitude gave her the opportunity to savour all the things she was learning for the first time in her life.

She thought again of Schliemann. What a strange man! And what an extraordinary life he had had! Born in Prussia a decade after that morning when Byron, on publication of *Childe Harold's Pilgrimage*, woke up to find himself famous, he was, unlike Byron, poor. Byron, who was a lord, sailed round the coasts of Greece and Turkey for pleasure in his twenties; Schliemann didn't get there till he was forty-six and had earned enough money for his travels.

When at last he came to Greece he set about acquiring, through a marriage bureau, a Greek wife, Sophia Engastromenos, who was still a schoolgirl. She was beautiful as well as intelligent, and must have been pretty tough as well, because she helped him in his excavations, all of which were reported in *The Times* and the *Daily Telegraph* of his day. Interest in his work was greatly increased when scandalous rumours began to circulate about the disappearance of the gold treasure dug up at Hisarcik in Turkey: diadems, bracelets and necklaces that, in the public imagination, might once have adorned Helen of Troy. It was suspected that Schliemann had poured them all into Sophia's jewellery box and smuggled it out of the country.

On Friday morning Ben said: 'I shall have to attend the farewell party tonight. Some music teachers are bringing their wives, and some parents are coming too.' He didn't need to tell Letty he couldn't invite her, lest any gossip about her presence with him in Athens might filter back to Bushbridge. The outside world was impinging on their glass bubble of bliss; it struck but did not shatter the surface.

'Don't worry about me!' cried Letty, waving a fat paperback. 'I shall be busy with *Zorba the Greek*! It's by the Cretan writer, Kazantzakis, you know.' He had been a freedom fighter too. She remembered reading somewhere the words on his tomb: *I fear nothing, I hope for nothing. I am free.*

'You don't mind being left out then?' he asked doubtfully. She was really a most independent woman; perhaps, he thought, from having been a single parent for so long. Celia, in a similar situation, for all her liberationist ideology, would not have taken the exclusion so calmly. With a why-not-me-too expression, and regardless of his feelings in the matter, she would have managed somehow to get there. Celia loved a party, so long as she didn't have to do any of the drudgery necessary to prepare one.

'But will you be able to get away in time to catch the night boat to Crete?' Letty asked. She had already booked the tickets. 'I could meet you on the quayside.'

'I'll attend the cocktail session and cut the rest,' he said. 'The booked tickets will let me off the dinner.'

'Well don't get drunk and miss the boat!' she warned him, before returning her attention to Zorba the patriot, a great, life-loving, earthy man, if ever there was one, bent on the evolutionary imperative to sow his genes far and wide.

She recognized him as a real menace to civilized female interests, but she couldn't help being fascinated by the rogue male. He would keep her amused till it was time to start that long night's voyage.

They intended sitting up all night on deck. It was the cheapest way to get to Crete, and they wanted to save what money they could to spend while on the island. It would probably be cold once the sun went down, but they would share a blanket, as well as the bottle of wine and the picnic she had prepared. They would stare up at the sky to watch a slim young moon swing in her hammock of night-blue silk among the god-named stars: Orion, the great hunter with three burnished buckles on his belt, Scorpio who killed that hunter with his poisoned sting, and Cassiopoeia, who, for boasting of her own beauty, was exiled to the heavens, there to sit for ever with arms raised in supplication to the unforgiving gods. Those old Greek gods were surprisingly hard-hearted to a pretty girl – certainly not as kind as Schliemann was to his Sophia. Letty thought she might tell Ben the story of Schliemann to pass the time that night.

'You folks having breakfast?' A young man, looking surprisingly fresh and cheerful after a night spent out on deck, addressed them as they stepped off the gangway. Ben looked him over morosely without replying, but Letty, though bleary-eyed from lack of sleep, tried to smile. The stranger had a pack on his back and a guitar slung across his chest, but his arms were free. Ben was already carrying two bags, and Letty was struggling with hers when the young man took it from her, explaining blithely:

'What I want right now is a cookie with goo in it.'

Ben considered him excessively naïve in his expectations, and was surprised, after a short bus-ride away from the port and into Venizelou Square in the centre of town, to find a café where such a cookie was indeed available. So it happened that they were all introduced to *bougatsa*: flaky pastry filled with a cream dusted with sugar and cinnamon, which when eaten with lots of strong, hot coffee, soon restored Ben to a more friendly frame of mind.

'Did you manage to sleep on the boat?' he asked.

'Yeah. I drank a bottle of *krasi*, and then rolled up in my sleeping bag. How about you?'

Letty and Ben had not fared so well. They'd found a bench of sorts under a lifeboat, and here they huddled together under their blanket, but only managed to sleep fitfully.

'You stopping here?' asked the backpacker.

'For a few nights,' Letty replied. 'We want to see Knossos and the ruins. What about you?'

'Oh, I'm not into culture. More into beaches and bikinis.' He would catch a green-and-yellow bus bound for the mountains, whose acres of heather and aromatic herbs scented the air for miles, where wild marjoram could be found, which was, he assured them, powerfully aphrodisiac. After that the south coast with many sheltered coves facing towards Africa and the sun . . . .

'Wonderful,' he said, 'for swimming and for sex.'

'Until the weather breaks,' said Ben.

The young man nodded: 'Yeah. Rain's heavy when it comes.'

Ben and Letty found a little hotel that fulfilled all their hopes. It was startlingly white in the morning sun; big pots of pink oleander still in flower flanked the doorway, and lilac-coloured bougainvillea spilled over a whitewashed archway leading to a yard, where a woman was hanging washing out to dry. Outside the window of their bedroom was a box containing scarlet geraniums; and what was even more attractive, the proprietor had reduced his prices, as the high season for tourists was over. They threw their bags on the bed and walked out into the sunshine.

'We'll go for culture tomorrow,'said Ben. 'Today we'll just wander, and get a feel of the place.'

'Soaked in blood,' said Letty. 'A bloody history.'

'Oh, absolutely full of horrors,' he agreed.

They smiled happily at each other.

In the afternoon, refusing to take their cue from mad dogs and Englishmen who insist on parading about in the midday sun, they retired like the locals for a siesta, and made love on their big, creaking bed, before falling asleep. They got up in the evening when it was cool, showered and dressed, and went out to join the *volta*, or evening promenade, stopping at small shops open to the pavement where eager sellers greeted them: *'Kalispera!'* But they decided to postpone the purchase of gifts till their last day on Crete, and bought only postcards. They found a pavement café where, in between scribbling greetings to friends and office colleagues, they could watch the world go by.

Ben liked the local *ouzo*, smelling of aniseed, with tasty aperitif morsels called *mezedes*, but Letty preferred a glass of cool white wine with a few slices of grilled octopus tentacle to chew on as she sipped.

'To my Teller of Tales!' said Ben, smiling at her across the little table.

'I'm too tired for any Arabian Nights,' she said. 'Tonight I can only manage tourists' titbits.'

'Such as . . .?'

'It says here,' she picked up her guide book, ' "that in spite of numerous rebellions by the Cretans the island was freed from the Turks only a hundred years ago".'

By the time they got back to their hotel they were both too sleepy for storytelling, too tired even for sex.

'I wonder,' murmured Ben as his head sank into his pillow, 'I wonder if that young fellow found any wild marjoram?'

'I don't think he needs much of that particular herb,' said Letty.

A small group from what must have been the last of the British summer package tours gathered round the bust of Sir Arthur Evans at the entrance to the ruins of the palace at Knossos. Ben and Letty stood in the background listening with half an ear to their guide. She was a handsome Greek lady, much more elegantly dressed than her hearers in their T-shirts and garishly printed shorts. Her white tunic was overlaid by a scarlet tabard decorated with what Letty guessed must have been Cretan embroidery, her well-cut black hair gleamed in the sunshine, and when she moved her head her long gold earrings glittered as they swung.

She pointed at the bust of the man who had discovered the site of the palace, and then unearthed remains of a sophisticated civilization that predated the ancient Greeks. 'An English gentleman archaeologist,' was how she described Arthur Evans. 'A Pommie Digger!' said an Australian voice in the crowd, and was rewarded by a few laughs.

They moved slowly through the ruins admiring the halls and corridors, the head of the sacred horned bull, the shrine of the Double Axes. The Double Axe logo was obviously a sacred symbol. Letty wondered about its significance. Was it the implement with which sacrificial animals were slaughtered on the altar? The Queen's apartment, decorated with a frieze of dolphins, was what roused the greatest interest and delight among the tourists, chiefly because of its ensuite bath-tub with toilet, complete with a water-flushing drainage system.

'Would you believe it possible?' Letty overheard one woman 'And it's about four thousand years old!'

But what Letty liked best were the *pithoi* standing outside the palace, giant pots used for storing grain, oil or wine. She put her arm round the neck of one, while the guide was looking the other way, and felt on her bare skin the warmth soaked up from the sun by the great terracotta jar.

'It's big enough to hide one of Ali Baba's forty thieves,' she said.

'Two of them,' said Ben, 'if the neck were wide enough to admit a man's shoulders.'

As she turned away her foot touched a plant growing between stones at the base of the jar.

'Oh, do look Ben!' she cried. 'I do believe it's a mandrake!'

He crouched down to examine its large leaves and its solitary fruit like a shiny orange egg.

'I believe it's supposed to shriek when pulled up by the roots,' he said.

'Certainly full of magic and medicine,' said Letty.

But it was not till they saw the original frescoes in the museum that Ben and Letty really felt the impact of the magical prehistoric Minoan world. The famous painting of the sport of bull-leaping, in which girls as well as boys took part, jumping on to the head of a charging animal and somersaulting over its back to safe ground behind, was a revelation.

'It must have been terribly dangerous,' remarked Ben.

'I suppose remnants of this sport can be seen in Spanish bull-fights, and perhaps that bull-running they do in Pamplona, for some festival or other,' said Letty. 'Perhaps the whole Mediterranean region was devoted to the bull religion once.'

'Well, it was fertility worship really,' said Ben.

The fresco of a procession led by a musician with lyre excited and delighted them as they tried to unravel its meaning in modern terms.

'Why, Ben, it's a Dance of the Girls with Lilies, isn't it?'

'I think they're men, Letty, not girls, although that priest, prince, or whoever it is leading the procession does wear a head-dress of lilies and a pretty collar of irises round his neck.'

'He's holding some animal and it's going to be sacrificed.'

'It's a procession.'

'But they seem to be dancing. It's a ritual dance.'

'It's a religious festival, or a celebration of something.'

'It's the rites of spring.'

Letty couldn't help wishing it was springtime now, so that she could see all these gorgeous flowers depicted on the fresco blooming in the wild; but at least, she consoled herself, she'd seen the mandrake plant. That was something to tell Isadora when she got home. And in her head Letty could already hear Isadora droning in her best RADA-trained accent: ' "*Not poppy nor mandragora / Nor all the drowsy syrups of the world / Shall ever medicine thee to that sweet sleep / Which thou ow'dst yesterday*".'

Of course they had to see the famous painted pottery figurine of a snake-charming goddess with her long full skirt of seven tiers of flounces and her naked breasts. She was holding at arm's length a pair of writhing snakes.

'She's like something topless out of *Vogue*,' said Letty.

'Well, I can't see a model nowadays holding snakes in her bare hands,' said Ben. 'I guess she was a priestess of some snake-worshipping cult. It says here they used to keep snakes in jars,' he read out in English from an explanatory label. 'And they fed them with milk.'

'Another dangerous sport,' said Letty. 'I must get a postcard of her for Jude.'

'I expect he's seeing lots of topless black beauties out in Angola.'

'You think so? Well, maybe I'll send it to Barney.'

'You don't think it might give the poor old boy ideas?'

'Barney has learned how to marshal his ideas.'

Ben picked up a postcard showing the bull-leaping athletes. 'I'll send that to Chris,' he said. 'There's enough activity there even for him.'

By the time they came to order lunch they were ready to try out a few more Greek words.

' Your health!' said Letty. '*Yasas!*'

'*Yamas!* To us!' said Ben.

They were eating *soutzoukakia*, or meat balls, with *melitsanasalata*, which was smoked aubergine, and enjoying it. Letty, who had rather a sweet tooth decided to try *baklava* for dessert, which proved to be a flaky pastry-case filled with honey and nuts, but Ben stuck to *ouzo* with his coffee.

'It's Sunday, you know,' he said. 'So shall we try the local Byzantine church this afternoon?'

'I'll have to put on a cardigan to cover my bare arms,' said Letty. 'I believe Greek churchgoers don't like to see bare skin.' She knew her legs would not arouse disapproval since she was wearing jeans.

The church of Ayios Titos was open but empty of worshippers, apart from a few old women dressed in black. A great iron candelabrum stood before an icon of the Virgin and Holy Child. Her white face was tilted stiffly in the traditional Byzantine style towards the infant resting on her arm, and behind her head the gold paint of her halo glittered in the light from flickering candles. Letty dropped a coin in the collecting-box, and lit a candle. As she did so Ben grasped her wrist so that both their hands together put the bright offering into its sconce. Letty glanced at him for one uncertain moment. Was he trying to hallow their union by joining their hands in a church?

'It's a sort of magic,' he explained, as they left the cool, incense-scented interior of the building for the bright air outside. 'Two hands joined in a burning prayer. A bit like the crossed double axes. That of course entailed a sacrifice,' he added, 'of more than a candle.'

'Well, those old Cretans were praying for fertility,' she said.

'We're not. All we're asking the gods is to keep the evil eye away from our love.'

They walked towards the harbour holding hands, and climbed to the top of the battlements of the Venetian fortress, into which, during one long siege, decapitated heads of prisoners of war were catapulted. They stopped now and again to look at all the ships anchored down below. Ben leaned over the wall and stared at the sea thoughtfully.

'I wonder what they were really like, those ancient Cretans,' he said. 'No written records of history or poetry. Into agriculture, of course, as well as bull worship. Good plumbers too, as well as handy with the paintbrush.'

'They seem to have loved life,' said Letty.

'Well, they certainly weren't Puritans.'

'Perhaps they were Rousseau's original unspoilt natural men who did no evil.'

'But there is that myth about feeding young men and maidens to the Minotaur. So they must have gone in for human sacrifice at one time. That's a bit evil, isn't it?' Archaeology had uncovered no signs of a love of military glory; they seemed to have been an unaggressive people. He supposed that this island race was primarily interested in trading. 'It must have been foreign invaders who turned them into wild mountain men and freedom fighters like the hero of your Zorba book,' he said.

'In the days when Titus was sent by St Paul to convert them to Christianity,' said Letty, 'he described them as "liars, evil beasts, and lazy gluttons".'

Ben nodded. 'Just like us, then; but enjoying a better climate.'

At breakfast on their last morning, as the waiter put coffee on the table, Ben remarked cheerfully:

'Aghios Nikolaus today.'

They wanted to spend their last day on the seashore, swimming and basking in the sun, with perhaps a picnic in some isolated cove, and were hoping to visit the resort famed for its beautiful bay in the Gulf of Mirabello as well as its modern amenities.

'Aghios Nikolaus too far,' said the waiter. 'Bad time coming.' And by way of explanation he added: 'Rain.'

'Rain today?' asked Ben anxiously.

The waiter lifted first one shoulder, then the other, in an attempt to excuse himself of all blame for the weather-change he knew to be imminent.

'Rain,' he repeated.

He must have read consternation on Ben's face, and described it in the kitchen, because a little later the proprietor's wife emerged and, wiping her hands on her apron as she bustled towards their table, she proceeded to tell them in broken English that her brother was delivering potatoes from the family farm that morning, that on his way back he could take them to the coast:

'Near Koutouloufari. Antic village. Beautiful as picture.

Plenty taverna.'

Letty nodded. They could shelter in a taverna if it rained.

'Is there any bus to bring us home?' she asked.

'Taxi,' said the proprietor's wife. 'Not far. Not too much money.' Her brother's friend owned a taxi.

Her brother drove them in a battered van, bypassing the village and driving at reckless speed through narrow lanes down to the shore, where he left them, promising that his friend would pick them up at 5 p.m. outside the taverna in Koutouloufari and return them to Heraklion 'for five per cent.'

There was no isolated cove to be seen on the long flat beach, and there were other swimmers, but it was not too crowded, and the sea was so warm it felt like silk on the skin. Ben wanted Letty to strip like the topless goddess of Knossos.

'You're just as beautiful as she is!' he declared.

'But there are too many people about!' she grumbled. She pushed out into the water till it was high enough to cradle her breasts, and then she pulled off her bikini top, while Ben swam round her in the shallow water, turning over on to his back so that he could see her more easily, thinking he couldn't remember a time when he'd been happier.

'You're behaving like a basking shark,' she said. 'And I feel menaced.'

She plunged into the water and swam away, laughing, till he caught and held her, and planting a kiss between the strands of wet hair on her shoulder blades, sank with her under the surface of the warm sea. They walked back hand in hand to the village taverna, where they ate a very leisurely lunch. This time it was fish, sea-bream freshly caught and grilled, and drank *retsina* with it, followed by black coffee and a delicious almond-flavoured sweet liqueur. They spent the rest of the afternoon exploring the cobbled main street, with all its many narrow alleyways, and lingered over open-air displays of goods set out to tempt the tourist. A stack of balloons in animal shapes caught their fancy, and Ben bought an octopus for Chris.

'It's bound to burst long before we get home,' said Letty, holding it by a string as the creature floated upwards, slowly wafting its many-coloured tentacles.

At that moment a man with a camera, holding a paper in his hand, ran up to them. He wanted to sell them a bad polaroid snap of Letty laughing as she dangled the octopus.

'Oh no!' she cried. 'It's awful. I look a fright!'

But Ben insisted on buying it. He never took a camera when he travelled for LUMCA. A camera was just one more thing to get lost or stolen, so he had no photo of her on this trip.

'I want it,' he said. 'It's lovely of you. So funny.'

They went back to the taverna to wait for Mister Five-per-Cent, and drank more coffee as they waited. Several times they glanced apprehensively at the sky, expecting to see rain-clouds; but no rain came.

It wasn't till they were in bed that night that a gust of wind suddenly blew open their window with a clatter, and rain, like a stutter of bullets, fell on the windowsill. Ben got out of bed to shut the window; and they listened to it drumming on the glass, steady, remorseless rain. Letty clung to him then, shivering a little as she was seized by sudden fear of impending loss of joy. Their brief honeymoon was over, and there was no happy marriage to look forward to. Tomorrow they would fly to Athens, and from there to England, back to the real world, and their separate lives.

'Darling,' she whispered. 'It's been the happiest time of my whole life. And thank you for it.'

But even as she spoke, her truthfully recording inner voice reminded her of Jude at four months, Jude in her arms, looking up at her after a feed, smiling and vocalizing his baby gratitude. How madly happy she had been then! She must have been in love. Mothers do fall in love with their babies. It was a special state of feeling humans had evolved to protect the delicate, vulnerable infant from harm, and though of course the intensity of that love was modified with time, it remained, she knew, rooted in the psyche.

'My little mermaid!' Ben said, running his fingers through strands of her hair still damp from the shower that had washed away the salt from the Sea of Crete. 'It's been a magical time.'

He thought of that other water-sprite, the legendary Undine, of what she had to suffer in order to leave her lake and gain a human soul with which to love her prince. Every time she moved on land a stab of pain shot through the legs she had exchanged for her fishtail; but her lover liked to see her dance, and so she danced for him while he sat on his throne beside the bride he'd chosen instead of her.

Ben pushed that image out of his mind. It was too sad to contemplate. And it was, after all, only a fairytale.

6

Celia was surprised by the violence of Ben's angry reaction when she showed him the corkscrew. Men usually took sexual innuendoes more lightly than women, she believed, so she expected him to laugh, telling her it was from some colleague at LUMCA envious of his trip to Athens.

'Just look at what some prankster sent me while you were away,' she said, handing the thing to him. But he didn't laugh. Instead he grew very red in the face, snatched it from her, examined it closely for a few seconds, and then blurted out:

'How disgusting! And to make it a lame girl too! That makes it worse. Evil really.' He threw it on the floor.

Celia picked it up and examined it again.

'Well, it wasn't made with a cracked hip-joint,' she remarked, rather stupidly. 'And no doubt it was cheaper to buy because it was damaged.'

What did he mean by a 'lame girl'? She supposed anyone with a crack in the thigh would be lame, but until that moment she hadn't given the object any human or personal qualities, had not thought of a girl at all. A lame girl? That was a strange idea of Ben's.

He went to the window, and stared out over the kitchen sink at the back garden where the grass needed a last cut before the winter. He'd have to be careful, he thought. He had nearly given the game away. He was naturally a truthful man, unused to checking his speech for lies, since he very rarely lied; but from now on he was, he knew, entering a life of deceit. He was following a forked way in which one path was the well-trodden one of his everyday existence, clear and open to inspection by anyone who chose to look, but the other, thronged with images of Letty, of memories of Crete, and his Sunday world with her in Alexandra Row, was the vivid tumultuous one that must remain hidden.

For the first time he was glad he didn't sleep with his wife. He might utter Letty's name in his dreams; and Celia would begin to ask questions: Who is Letty? Teasing him about the existence of a pretty student or secretary at LUMCA ... And that horrible object! Of course it must be the Crinkham woman who'd sent it. She would have picked it up at the antiques market where she was always nosing and rummaging about, and bought it cheaply because of the damaged joint. He imagined her laughing because the fractured joint was so apt. But why on earth should she go to such lengths of malice to strike him? Though she probably guessed he regarded her as an eccentric, he had never, as far as he could remember, been rude or unkind to her. So why did she hate him?

He turned away from the window and spoke as lightly as he could:

'I wonder if it's a rare antique object? *Erotica antiqua*. The Victorians had their own style of pornography, for all their family values! But like all pornography, rather crude .... Harmless really; but better not let Chris see it.'

Celia stood with her hand outstretched, and the thing still in it. 'Oh no, of course not! What do you think I should do with it?'

'Throw it away. Get rid of it. It was just somebody's little lewd joke in bad taste. Forget it.'

For a few days she did forget about it; but she didn't throw it away, partly because she was still wondering about its origins, and partly because, being a frugal housewife she didn't care to throw what might be a not altogether valueless thing into the dustbin. So she pushed it away into one of the drawers of her desk. She did not at first suspect that it could be in any way connected with that odd phone call from the travel agent about booking a double room with a view of the Acropolis. It was Ben's sudden anger, the unexpected violence of his reaction when she showed him the thing, that, like a stone in the sole of a shoe, rubbed at her consciousness, till on Saturday afternoon, when she was doing the washing-up, because Ben was loyally watching Chris play football with his school team, the three incidents hooked together in her mind to form a small suspicion.

Celia had never installed a washing-up machine in the kitchen. She regarded it (except for use in restaurants or hotels) as wasteful, since it needed such large quantities of energy and water to do a job that Ben could do more simply, quickly and cheaply with his hands; but as Ben was away that Saturday, looking after Chris, it was her duty to do it. Now her movements at the sink slowed down, her eyes, unfocused, gazed at a cup she was wiping as she asked herself: Could Ben possibly be having an affair? And was there someone who, for unknowable personal reasons was trying to warn her of it? She continued wiping the cup with a brush, over and over again. Was this really happening? She couldn't believe it.

As soon as they returned from the school playing-field Chris threw his gear on the kitchen floor and ran upstairs to his bedroom to fetch the floating octopus his Dad had brought him back from Greece. Celia noticed, as Ben sat down at the table, that he looked a bit morose. She made a pot of tea for them both, and sat down opposite him.

'Everything all right?' she asked.

He nodded; but said nothing for a few minutes. Then he began to grumble in what to Celia seemed a long, rambling monologue: 'Plainchant's OK when sung by disciplined, highly trained monks in a great stone abbey, you know, with a vast vaulted roof where the sound can reverberate; but it's another matter when it has to be dragged out of the throats of a bunch of boys who hate the dryness of it, the coldness and lack of melody. It's just sounds scratched into the air then.'

'I'm sure you're right,' said Celia soothingly. 'But why all this? Are they going to introduce plainchant at St Augustine's?'

'Unfortunately, yes.' Ben gazed past his wife through the window at the still uncut grass, and thought of the other evening when Father Gregory had drawn him aside after choir practice.

'Have you a moment to spare, Ben?'

He led him to his study where he seemed to have all the time in the world to spare, offering him a *copita* of his best and driest *Tio Pepe*, and only then revealing that a new young priest, who would be taking over the choir, wanted to introduce plainchant.

'Time I went, I suppose,' he said ruefully.

'You're not old enough to retire, surely?' Ben was indignant; but his objection was waved aside.

'I shall be sorry to go. More than sorry about losing you, too, old chap, after so many years. He's mad about plainchant, this young Turk; and of course we don't need the organ for that. But there'll always be high mass to celebrate feast days, Christmas, Easter, Whitsun, you know. We'll hear your splendid chorales blowing forth from the organ loft then.'

Shock and dismay had made Ben swallow his *Tio Pepe* in a single philistine gulp. When he said nothing Father Gregory continued quickly:

'Sorry old chap. I couldn't do much about it, you know. St Augustine's, it seems, has run into terrible trouble with the bankers. School subsidies to the church have been cut. They're even going to admit girls to classes in order to raise more fees. The auditors are pruning everything. We seem to have been sailing along in some sort of eccelesiastical Titanic, blissfully blind; but now we've hit an iceberg everything's being cut. Everything. All sorts of economies. You'd never guess. It seems we've even been too extravagant with heating and lighting. When winter comes we'll all be shivering as we sing.'

'Sherry's good,' said Ben, wondering if he'd just swallowed the last of it before that too was cut, and thinking plainchant was enough to make them all shiver without the loss of heating. 'So are we just enjoying a last drink before the ship goes down? Are things really so dire?'

'Dire!' said Father Gregory. 'Absolutely dire!' He sighed noisily. 'As a matter of fact it'll be worse than plainchant if the boys can't cope with that. There'll be no music at all then. It'll be low mass not only in Advent and Lent but most of the summer too.' He sipped, and *Tio Pepe* seemed to lighten his gloom. 'But you'll still be needed for feast days, as I explained, and of course for weddings and funerals as before.'

*

'You know, Celia,' Ben said, 'I've never liked plainchant much myself.' He found it difficult to understand why this early music was suddenly so popular that, according to commercial surveys of CD sales, it had shot right to the top of the pop charts. He himself often gave thanks for Palestrina, who got church music out of the punitive plainchant doldrums of the Middle Ages into what he considered a kinder, more harmonious mode. Of course he could appreciate up to a point the cold beauty of what the Solesmes choir could produce with the acoustic properties provided by their great abbey: the rise and fall of notes, the smooth phrasing, the short pause for an intake of breath, the absolutely faultless unison. It was a performance of military precision impossible to achieve with bored, rebellious schoolboys, who would be able to detect in the music no regular rhythm, nor any catchable tune.

And what, Ben asked himself angrily, were those monks of Solesmes singing for anyway? The glory of God. *Laudate Dominum*. Praise the Lord. To praise with suffering, to chastise the senses, was that what it was for? Did God really want such bleak praise?

Celia poured him out a second cup of tea, saying: 'Even with Gregorian chant they'll need the organ before the Introit. Won't they? And perhaps for the *Ite Missa Est* to send off the congregation at the end of mass.'

'I think they're trying to save money by cutting out my services.'

'Oh surely not!' She clattered her cup briskly on its saucer, adding cheerfully: 'Well, there's always a bright side to these things. You know what they say: "When one door closes another opens". So even if you do lose some Sunday sessions at St Augustine's you can always come down to Uckfield with us. Daddy and Mummy would be pleased to see you. They often ask me when you're going to come.'

Ben scowled. He didn't relish the prospect of Sunday sessions with Daddy and Mummy in Uckfield. And he couldn't explain that, much as he disliked the inevitable loss of fees it was the possible reduction in the number of Sundays when he could hold Letty in his arms that he dreaded most.

Chris came swaggering into the kitchen swinging the mobile octopus on its elastic and demanding his Saturday doughnut. He sat down, placing the creature on his head, letting its tentacles dangle round his face, and grinning. Celia frowned at him, but full as he was of that special euphoria the young feel after hard physical exercise, he was not to be subdued.

'He scored a goal today,' said Ben, laughing and eager to share his son's elation; but Celia said in her most commanding voice:

'Put that beastly animal under the table.'

'He's not an animal.'

'Well fish then.'

'He's not a fish either.'

'Well, what is he, I'd like to know?'

Silence. Then Celia in her firmest voice:

'Put that Greek pest under the table or you'll not get any doughnut. And where's Sarah?'

Sarah was lost in the *Tales from the Arabian Nights* which she was reading while lying on her bed, and had forgotten tea till Ben called out from the hall:

'Sarah? Sarah! Doughnuts!' Then she threw her book on the ground, seized the tiny bottle of perfume Daddy had bought for her at a duty free shop on his travels, and she dabbed some proudly on her neck. She was specially proud because Mummy had rebuked him, saying: 'She's much too young for French perfume, Ben!' Mummy didn't know a thing. She didn't know, for instance, that her daughter was going to marry a tyrant. Like Scheherezade Sarah was going to calm his savagery by telling him wonderful stories every night, and when she couldn't think of any more stories a few dabs of the French perfume would make him fall in love with her and forget all about chopping off her head. She felt a delicious little shiver of fear as she touched her neck and thought of the tyrant's knife.

'Coming, Dad!' she shouted, and then ran quickly down the stairs.

Celia liked to be certain about things; she didn't like living with doubts; but November with its uncertain weather and its unpredictable swings of temperature was increasing her uneasiness, making her own moods swing from one uncertainty to another. On cold foggy mornings when, sitting hunched over the driving-wheel of the car and peering through the clouded windscreen as she drove the children to school, she asked herself: Who can she be, this woman? But when at noon a sudden blaze of sunshine cleared the mist in the college garden, where she was taking a brisk walk during lunch break, and she saw hedges bedecked with cobwebs like jewelled necklaces, all their fine filigree hung with droplet diamonds reflecting light, she smiled, telling herself she was imagining things. Ben would never dare to be so foolish. He had too much to lose. And anyway, she didn't believe he would ever be so selfish; nor was he really capable of doing anything so romantic as having a passionate affair. She rather wished he would do something exciting for once – the staid old thing! And she laughed to herself.

But when evening came, the temperature dropping as darkness fell, and she had to drive home in a crawling centipede of traffic, through a confusion of blurred headlights as her windscreen wipers scraped monotonously, left right, left right, before her eyes, clearing away the mud-spatterings from the wheels of the car immediately in front of hers, she thought: Well, damn and blast him to hell if it's true! And as she settled down to sleep at night nagging suspicions returned to trouble her. Somebody had sent her those queer messages. Somebody knew more than she did. She tried to construct in her imagination possible scenarios of a love affair for Ben. It must be some girl up at LUMCA, some young independent woman living in a bedsit in London. But when did they make love? His work timetable was so full he had no leisure time by day, and he was almost never away from home in the evenings. The only time he could not be under her scrutiny was on Sundays when he was at Milton-on-the-Mount. But whom could he have met there in that all male society at St Augustine's? Some good pious lady who arranged the flowers? Perhaps someone from Toni's, where Ben went for lunch? A waitress perhaps, young and plump and giggly? Or a single lady luncher he'd fallen into conversation with . . .? Even playing the organ in a church could be the pathway to adultery, she supposed, though it all seemed somehow a bit unlikely.

Gradually the uncertainty became more difficult to bear, till she determined to find out the truth. But how? It was probable, she reasoned, that as he couldn't see this person very often he would be corresponding with her, no doubt phoning her when he was away from home, but perhaps by letter, and if so there would be written evidence somewhere until it was destroyed.

She began to inspect wastepaper baskets and dustbin for torn letters, feeling so ashamed that after each search through litter she would wash her hands carefully to remove the smell of her dirty action. She began to watch where he hung his jacket, suspecting that an incriminating letter might be hidden in one of his pockets; but it wasn't easy to look without letting Ben know what she was up to. Since they slept in separate rooms he hung up his clothes in his own separate cupboard; when he left his bedroom they went with him on his back.

But one evening when it was unusually warm for November he threw his jacket over the banisters in the hall before going into his music-room, where he sat down at the piano and began to play a Beethoven sonata. Celia knew it would be about twenty minutes before he finished it; the children were doing their homework in her study; there was no one about to see her; suddenly the chance to discover the truth presented itself.

For a moment she hesitated. She had never before demeaned herself by prying in other people's pockets, but now the urge to know for certain pushed aside her shame as she began to pick through one pocket after another, only to be disappointed. There was no letter to be found. But on opening his wallet a faded polaroid photo fell out on to the lowest step of the stairs, and slid slowly to the floor.

From where she stood she could see it was of a girl dangling a toy octopus. She was afraid that if she moved the floorboards might creak, but very carefully she stooped and lifted the picture towards the light. Well now she did know. It was all immediately clear to her. This was the girl who went with him to Greece, a woman still-young with a lot of brown hair, wearing a green trouser suit. Nothing to write home about; but she was laughing. Yes, she did look happy.

Celia examined the photo more intently. She knew that look. It was happiness, the sort of happiness that Celia hadn't felt in years. The girl was in love. That knowledge stabbed her so sharply that she sat down suddenly on the stairs. Her stomach was being powerfully squeezed, as rage mounted and rushed around her head, making her tremble. What she ought to do was to march calmly into the music-room with this tacky polaroid and slam the piano lid down on Ben's fingers, demanding: Who the hell's this doxy of yours? She might surprise and shame him into confession. Or he might lose his temper and shout. Then their voices raised in anger and the sudden stopping of the piano would bring the children running into the hall crying: 'What's the matter?' That wouldn't be right, upsetting them like that. Or he might deny everything, scolding her for shameful snooping, perhaps laughing at her for her use of the word 'doxy', saying: 'Doxy? I don't think they exist any more. Died out with *Tom Jones*, didn't they?' She would look foolish then, she knew.

And she might be wrong. Had she really any proof? The whole story she had dreamed up was unbelievable. And perhaps, after all, she told herself, she shouldn't believe it. What about the benefit of the doubt, and being innocent till proven guilty? This girl might just be the saleswoman who sold Ben that toy. Perhaps Greek salesgirls smiled like that, ingratiatingly, in order to sell toy octopuses to foreign tourists.

She replaced the photo in Ben's wallet, and the wallet in the breast pocket of his jacket. She was, she realized, no more certain after than before her spying. What she was left with was a slow-burning anger of humiliation when she thought that, if he was having an affair, he'd taken so little trouble to cover his traces. Leaving this photo in his wallet like that just showed how little he valued her intelligence. He was a stupid deceiver, (if deceiver he was) and she despised him for it. And then she argued with herself that perhaps the very fact that he'd been so careless might be because he was innocent.

As November moved on towards Christmas she began to long for the holidays in order to sleep. She had never before felt so tired. She went to bed earlier, but woke in the small hours with bad dreams. It was then that she saw Ben as an adulterer; but when in the morning at breakfast he was his usual affable self, his appetite unimpaired, his manner to the children still kind and humorous, his attitude to his work unruffled, she thought: Of course not! He is really the ideal husband! But by evening it only added to her anger to see him so serene a sinner (if that's what he was,) while she, the innocent, injured wife, should be suffering this erosion of self-confidence, this loss of equanimity that was making her snap at the children, hurt her pupils with too sarcastic put-downs, impatient with colleagues who were harrying her with tasks and questions, and coldly distant with Ben. She began to feel as if her world were collapsing on top of her, pushing her down with the weight of all those duties that once had seemed such a light and pleasant burden to carry.

It was her nightmare that made her certain of the truth at last. It must have been 4 or 5 a.m. when she woke, to the sound of laughter, her heart racing, her mouth open as if she'd just uttered a cry. She had been running along a narrow alleyway, trying to catch a girl who was holding in her hand something that Celia desperately needed. The girl was laughing, and as they drew level she looked back over her shoulder and said: 'It's love you know. The real thing.'

Celia sat up in bed and let the shreds of sleep fall away from her. She felt ill. She pressed her face against her hands. She was in no narrow alleyway but in the bedroom of her own house in the middle of the night. Jealousy is my disease, she thought. The worm in the bud. She remembered Blake: *O Rose thou art sick* .... The invisible worm that flies in the night is devouring me. So it was really Blake who made her decide to visit Dr Corrigan. He would give her something to help her sleep. Sleep, blessed sleep would cure this fatigue that was devouring all her energy. If she could only sleep she might be able to cope with Christmas.

From behind his desk Dr Corrigan examined Celia and decided she looked a bit older than when he'd last seen her. Her face seemed thinner, and there were dark shadows under her eyes. He glanced up at the brief précis of her medical history on his computer screen. Nothing more than a few notes about her two pregnancies. No complications there. Cervical smear and breast check a year ago both OK. She looked unhappy. He supposed she was about to join the long procession haunting his surgery of disappointed women, who having been brought up in relative ease compared with women in the developing world, and having consumed large quantities of romance from novels, the cinema and television, discovered that real life and real loving were not what they'd been taught to expect. Celia surely was not quite like that, he reminded himself. She was some sort of feminist, with a career of her own, and a husband in Ben who was what the Bible called a 'helpmeet'. She might belong to the sisterly solidarity, but she was certainly not all womb and wobbly thinking. You could never call her silly; she was so sensible, reasonable and efficient. He looked at her again. He must be careful not to miss the organic disease that even disappointed women may suffer from.

'It's not often I have the pleasure of seeing you in the surgery, Celia,' he said. 'What's the trouble?'

That old-fashioned courtesy hid a wily mind, Celia knew. She met his eye and thought: I wonder if I ought to spill the beans.

'I was hoping you'd give me something to help me sleep,' she said. 'Overwork, I suppose. I've been sleeping badly lately.'

'Troubles at college?'

'Troubles everywhere,' she replied gloomily, adding hastily: 'You've only to read the papers . . .'

'I expect it's your time of life, Celia. Things don't look so rosy then, as in our first youth.'

But Celia wasn't going to lie down under a sweepingly simplistic male chauvinist diagnosis of that sort.

'Certainly not!' she objected crossly. 'I've not yet reached my menopause. My periods are perfectly regular and trouble free.'

'Is there some other worry then?'

She was silent for a moment. In spite of her initial resolve to keep her secrets to herself she was tempted to confide in him. He was after all a man as well as a doctor; he might throw a different light on her uncertainties. She hesitated, and then before she could stop herself she blurted out:

'I suspect Ben's having an affair; but I'm not sure. It would be easier if I knew for certain.'

Dr Corrigan wrapped the sphygmomanometer sleeve round her arm and checked her blood pressure. 'Normal,' he said, and went on: 'Has he changed towards you, then?' His voice was gentle. 'Perhaps he makes love to you less often because he's older. That doesn't necessarily mean a lessening of love, you know.'

'Oh no. It's not that at all,' she said quickly. 'In any case we haven't slept together for years.'

'You sleep in separate rooms?' He tried not to show surprise.

'Well, yes. We couldn't afford any more children. And I wanted to get back to work. So we agreed.'

And what, Dr Corrigan was asking himself, what happened to the kindness of women on their way to liberation? That poor devil Ben Fording! He wondered how many years he'd been put out to celibate grass. He remembered that Celia had recently joined his church, and supposed she was having the scruples about contraception that all good Catholics torment their consciences with, and she, being a convert, would be more conscientious than most. Converts, he knew, were a bit inclined to fanaticism; they didn't have the common sense of cradle Catholics. In his own opinion the good Lord had more to worry about than a few condoms when he looked down from heaven and counted the millions of heads of population swarming over the surface of his world.

But no, he told himself, Celia had mentioned 'years' of separation in their sleeping arrangements, so that must have predated her conversion. It was obviously more than a dislike of contraceptives. Dr Corrigan wondered what to say next.

'What makes you think he's having an affair?' he asked at last.

Celia drew out of her handbag an object which she unwrapped from tissue paper and handed to him over the desk. He couldn't help laughing when he saw the corkscrew.

'An anonymous donor sent it to me,' she said.

'Oh, I see.' He tried to look grave. 'Well, that does put a rather different colour on it.'

She told him about the odd phone call, which might or might not have come from the tourist agency; she told him about the toy octopus Ben brought back for Chris, and the photo of the girl holding it that she'd found in his wallet.

'Well, it does look bad, I admit,' he said. 'But I suppose there could be other interpretations. Have you confronted Ben with your suspicions?'

'No.'

He met her eyes over his semi-lunar specs.

'Why don't you just go to him and say: "I'm worried. Will you tell me the truth and put me out of my misery? Are you having an affair with another woman, or not?" '

Celia didn't reply, twisting her hands in her lap. She wished she could go to Ben as simply as that, but the long years of lack of communication between them silenced her now.

'I feel I'm losing control of my own life,' she said.

'What do you feel about the matter yourself?' he asked. 'Wives usually know the truth, I believe.'

'I think he's having an affair,' she said, and quickly glanced down at her hands.

'These things don't last, you know,' he said. 'It might be best, after all, to say nothing, and let it all pass over. If you accuse him you might push him into the drastic step of leaving you and the children. But he wouldn't do that, would he? If you keep a low profile and simply remain silent for a while the affair will probably die a natural death. And in a year or two it will be safely in the past.' He added, when she made no response to his suggestion: 'It's a hard path to take, I know, when what you want to do is beat him over the head with your umbrella.'

She laughed then. 'That's one thing I don't have, an umbrella.'

He wrote out a prescription for one dose each night for a week, and then one for whenever she couldn't get to sleep, twenty capsules in all. He didn't want her to become addicted to the hypnotic.

He watched her back as she left the room, and felt a twinge of pity for her, a tall, straight woman with a fine pair of legs. In the Middle Ages she might have been an abbess, learned and saintly, ruling her convent with a firm hand, giving a purpose and a refuge to those others who, for whatever reason, didn't want to live in the world. In that era her desire for celibacy would have been regarded as holy; now it was unholy because of what, it seemed to him, it was doing: breaking up a perfectly good marriage and possibly fracturing the lives of her young children.

He sighed. Times changed; morality shifted. What mattered in the end was pain, its relief a virtue, infliction of it a vice. Even the Infallibility in Faith and Morals he'd learned to trust in his own childhood could no longer be relied on. What had seemed right in one century was beginning to look wrong in another.

And perhaps, after all, these small scruples of conscience besetting little human lives were of no consequence. If divine Providence were simply looking on while evolution took its course then it was really of no importance whether Celia, and others like her, curbed their fertility or not. In time the very success of the human species in its struggle for survival would be the cause of its extinction, when the surface of the globe was so pressed all over by human feet that not a blade of corn nor a potato could grow through it.

And who knows? That might well be part of the divine plan. We human creatures might in evolutionary terms be of no more importance than the dinosaurs. 'You exaggerate Patrick,' was what Celia would have said in her calm, reasonable voice, had he expressed these imaginings to her. All she'd wanted was to stop having babies in order to provide better for her family as a whole; but her plan had gone badly wrong. And Ben, poor devil, how had he been faring in all this denial of his body's needs? For years, was what she'd said.

He glanced again at the screen. That second child was born seven and a half years ago. He guessed it must have been after that that abstinence of the flesh had been forced upon her husband. Wasn't it that which had made him look for consolation from another woman?

Dr Corrigan couldn't help reflecting that in all the years he'd known the Fordings he'd had no inkling of what was going on. How little he knew about his patients' real lives! And now, when he had a drink with Ben at Christmas he'd have to pretend he knew nothing about the matter. He sighed again. The surgery was becoming more like the confessional every day! He pressed the buzzer for the next patient with some irritation, and glared at the poor woman quite unjustifiably as she entered and sat down.

7

It was going to be the best Christmas ever, Letty promised herself, as she put the last touches to her festive table in the little dining-room. All the carols for the early evening children's service at St Augustine's must by now have been sung, and the children's visits to the crib to see the baby Jesus asleep in his manger, to light candles and to pray for the Christmas presents of their dreams must all be ended.

Any minute now Ben would arrive. Not only was he going to be able to stay with her all night after the midnight mass on Christmas Eve, but Jude was going to phone her on Christmas Day from headquarters. She tried to calculate when the call would come. Greenwich Mean Time, rotating with the globe, must reach Jude hours ahead of London, Angola being so far away, she reckoned, and was surprised to find that the time difference was only one hour. She studied the map he'd pinned up on the kitchen wall, and saw that he was actually in the same longitude as Austria and southern Italy. He didn't seem so far away then.

Her Christmas celebrations would have to take place on

Christmas Eve, because Ben would have to leave on Christmas morning. No trains would be running, but Father Gregory, who was to spend the day with his sister in Sussex, would drive him down as far as Uckfield, where Celia would meet them and carry Ben off to her parents' house.

Letty thought a lot about Celia nowadays, wondering what sort of a woman she was. Ben didn't talk much about her, so Letty's picture of her was a guesswork collage. But she did sometimes fear that Celia would find out about her husband's affair, would suddenly explode the marriage with rage and jealousy and demand a divorce, which Ben didn't want because he didn't want to lose his children. Well, of course, they had to come first; they had to be protected; everyone knew the long-lasting damage loss of a parent did to a child.

And she herself, in similar circumstances, would have stood by Jude, first and last. But if the affair did come to such a crisis she would go to Celia; she would beard the lioness in her den and speak honestly: *Look. I don't want to break up your marriage. That would hurt the children.* They would talk things over calmly and reasonably. She certainly wouldn't heap garbage on Celia's head, informing her with angry screams that she was an inadequate mate, nor would she create a melodramatic scene as she implored an implacable wife for mercy, declaring that this love between herself and Ben was the biggest thing in both their lives, a passion they would die for, an absolutely paramount emotion demanding the sweeping aside of all other persons and considerations.

No. She would reassure Celia that she had no intention of stealing her husband, the father of her children, the sharer of her house and mortgage and part-provider of the family food stores. She would explain that Ben himself didn't want to break up the marriage, didn't want to lose his children, couldn't in any case, (since his profession and his wage-earning were tied up so securely to his piano in the music-room of his home in Bushbridge) for practical reasons, do so. All Letty wanted was Ben on Sunday afternoons. Surely it was not so much to ask for that part of Celia's life that had already been discarded and put out into their spare room?

The little prole from Chaplin's Walk came round to the kitchen at midday on Christmas Eve.

'Scrounging,' Isadora said.

But Letty regarded it as part of the child's struggle for survival.

'Even worms must eat, I suppose,' said Isadora.

'I've set him to cleaning my set of silver teaspoons,' said Letty defensively. 'And his name is Wayne.'

He had devoured two slices of Welsh rarebit and a mince-pie while polishing the spoons. Letty knew he had no full-time father, and his mum, though loving enough, didn't seem to know her arse from her elbow when it came to feeding time.

'She's a fucking witch,' he said as Isadora left the kitchen.

'Witch she may be,' agreed Letty. 'But I don't think she's fucking. What do you mean by that word anyway?'

'Bad,' he said, and repeated: 'bad bad.'

'Well, there are lots of words for bad, you know. There's wicked, rotten, mouldy, nasty, dirty, sinful, unpleasant, evil. And fucking's not really any of those things.'

'Yeah? She's fucking evil to me all right,' said Wayne.

Letty went into the dining-room to finish decorating the table for her candle-lit tea. It was to be a festive meal of cold sliced ham and turkey served with a salad of diced celery, chopped apple and hazel nuts, followed by hot mince-pies with brandy butter, and litle dishes of Isadora's special damson mousse.

Ten plump Santa Claus figures made of red apples, their faces painted on to walnut heads with long cotton-wool beards, each flanked by a scarlet candle, stood in a ring around her central arrangement of holly-twigs and winter-jasmine sprays. Places were laid with a scarlet napkin to each place, and teacups and saucers ready to receive their respective spoons.

At one end of the table stood Letty's Christmas cake covered with snowy icing through which sprouted little fir trees, and a Father Christmas figure, complete with sledge, ploughed an endless furrow. The cake was encircled by scarlet candles not yet lit. Letty was not going to allow much drinking because Ben had to play the organ later that evening for midnight mass, but since Isadora had provided a bottle of luscious sweet Sauterne given her by her niece as a Christmas present, that would be relished with the desserts.

Isadora was placing wineglasses on the table when Barney entered the room, followed closely by Wayne.

The boy's jaw fell when he saw the table, and his eyes focused on the red-apple Father Christmases with a kind of longing as he sighed: 'Cor!'

Barney could feel the boy's excitement; and Barney, too, stood stunned by the sight of the apples transfigured into myth, as out of the past another image suddenly flooded his vision.

Leipzig railway station. A train standing at the platform, its engine steaming. Not their train. He is standing with a crowd of British POWs, cold, hungry, half-asleep on his feet, tired almost to death of waiting for the trucks to take them to yet another POW camp, when he hears two sharp cracks. A sudden lull falls, not complete silence, for the gentle steaming of the engine can still be heard, but a cessation of activity, as if the station is holding its breath, as a procession of ragged, half-starved prisoners passes down the platform to the trucks reserved for them. He can hear the shuffling of feet in makeshift cloth boots, and see ankles chained with some metal, strong enough to prevent escape but not heavy enough to impede the swift movement required of them under the lash.

They are not Jews, but Polish slaves. The woman who sidles up to him must have seen his mouth open in a silent cry, must have read the terror on his boyish face and been filled with pity for him. Barney doesn't see her, doesn't know if she is German or Polish, but he notices the rough red hand above a skirt as she drops her red apple into his pocket. She moves away before he can thank her, before he can raise his eyes even to see her face.

Remembering now that act of kindness from a stranger so many years ago, Barney leaned forward and picked a Santa Claus out from its magic circle.

'May I, Letty?' he asked.

'Why yes,' she said. 'I have one or two more to take his place.'

Barney presented it to Wayne. 'It's for you,' he said.

'For me?' asked the boy in disbelief.

'Yes, take it,' Letty said. 'And before you go, there's a Christmas stocking for you under the tree in the hall. It's labelled "Wayne".'

'And you'll find a present from me wrapped in green paper there too,' called Isadora from the sideboard, where she was scooping spoonfuls of her damson mousse into small glass dishes.

Her voice checked him as he ran out into the hall. He turned his head to look at her, the shock of surprise pushing him into gratitude. 'Thanks,' he said. 'Thanks a lot.'

He snatched his presents from the foot of the tree, dislodging in his haste a paper angel and making a tiny glass bell tinkle before he fled, fearing this unexpected luck might vanish.

Ben was delighted that not only Letty but also Barney and Isadora were seated in the nave below the organ loft in order to attend midnight mass. As he eased himself into the suitably ornate-for-the-occasion motet by César Franck he had chosen as an introduction to the service he reflected that this was in reality his farewell to St Augustine's. It was the end of the year, and the end of the old regime for him. In the New Year there would be very few sung masses, and very little need for an organist, and that meant fewer opportunities for his seeing Letty.

The sadness of that reflection was soon dispelled by the sweet polyphony of William Byrd's Mass for Three Voices sung in this instance by three groups of voices from the choir. He was especially glad that Letty was there to hear it with him, and the harmonies of the Introit calmed his anxious heart.

He thought, as he listened to the clear, untroubled boys' voices, of how that music must originally have been performed in the days of good Queen Bess: in secrecy, in the small, intimate chapel of some rich Catholic recusant's house, in fear of betrayal and discovery by Burghley's spies, of torture and a horrid death for the priest at the makeshift altar, were he to be caught before he could be hidden in the hole in the wall prepared for him and later sumggled into another safe house. But that quiet music, so full of the certainty of faith, of absolute confidence in the good- ness of God, must have given the believers strength to endure.

Yes, life in those days was filled with terrible fears, but could be faced with faith in the benevolent providence of bliss beyond the grave, whereas in our own times we have exchanged fear of torture and imprisonment for following a treasonable religion, and a shorter lifespan for all men whatever their persuasion, for a long life full of uneventful Mr Prufrock days measured out with uneventful coffee spoons, of many disappointments, and no surety whatsoever for survival after it.

Ben turned away from these morose thoughts as he thun- dered out the melody of the carol at the end of mass, *0 Come All Ye Faithful*, while the whole congregation sang. That was what united them, gave them that warm Christmassy feeling of belonging to the religion of love and protection for the weak, the suffering and all the fall-outs from the struggle in our money-loving, power-targeted century, a faith symbolized by the adoration of the fragile body of the infant Christ.

Ben drew the cork of his bottle of 'champagne', legally only sparkling fizz, from a new vineyard down under. 'I want you all to try this,' he said. 'Full of the Australian sun, and as good as the true French in my opinion.'

They sat down rather formally in the sitting-room, which had grown cold after the central heating had switched itself off, and touched glasses, wishing each other happy Christmasses. When Ben touched Isadora's he tried to feel goodwill towards her, but although she smiled vaguely she wouldn't meet his eye. She feels guilty, he thought, she *is* guilty; and she must know that

Celia would have shown me that corkscrew, and that I would have guessed who sent it. What she doesn't know is that I've not told Letty anything about it for fear of her worrying about Celia's suspicions and feelings, and that wouldn't help anybody. So it was a secret he shared only with Isadora, and as they clinked glasses her eyes slithered away from his.

It was nearly 3 a.m. by the time she left with Barney, but Ben and Letty sat on the sofa a little while longer to finish the champagne.

'I don't like to think of your being alone tomorrow,' he said. Barney was to be picked up by his son in the morning and taken off for the day, and Isadora had an invitation to join Mrs Blum's Christmas dinner at Number 6.

'Oh, I shall be quite OK,' Letty said. 'I shall be waiting for Jude's phone call. That's the loveliest Christmas present he could give me. And Isadora will drop in for tea and Christmas-cake later in the day.'

Ben stroked the hollow of her back through her dress with his free hand, and held the lovely firm round buttock as he kissed her.

'Bed,' he said. 'Barney isn't the only one who's got to be up early. Father Gregory is going to pick me up soon after eight. And I don't want him to see me undressed.'

Barney and Isadora lingered in the garden. It was a clear crisp night, and he was searching in the sky for the Great Bear and the Pole Star. Both had been visible up on the Mount above the green spaces of the common, but down here in the town the light-pollution from street-lamps and the night-long flickering of neon advertisements above shops not far away obliterated them. He liked seeing the stars shining in their expected places in the firmament. Though individual human lives were ephemeral, and even the existence of the whole human race probably transient, it was a reassuring fact that even as the earth whirled through its annual cycles the stars remained at their stations.

'They're settling into being a regular married couple,' he said, coming back to earth.

'The man is not an itinerant lover,' Isadora granted. 'I will say that for him.'

'You never managed to wreck the affair after all, did you?'

'Whatever made you imagine I'd want to do such a thing?'

He nodded. 'Well, have a good dinner with Mrs Blum. She might be interested in buying a few small antiques.'

'Do you think so?' she murmured. She didn't like his mention of antiques. She felt herself floundering in uncertainties. Did Barney, too, know about the corkscrew? Only if Ben or Letty had told him. Perhaps they were all laughing at her behind her back. It was mortifying to contemplate the possibility.

After Ben left her Letty tried to occupy herself with household chores: washing up, tidying the bedroom, putting away the clean crockery and dusting the sitting-room, all the time with one ear listening for the phone, and one eye watching the clock; but the hours passed, and the phone didn't ring. She told herself it was almost certainly impossible for Jude to keep to a strict timetable out there in Angola. Perhaps he had to make his way in a jeep for miles to reach a telephone; perhaps the jeep had broken down and help was slow in coming; perhaps all lines of communication with home were simply overloaded with

Christmas greetings from abroad. There was time enough yet for him to ring. But by the time Isadora arrived for her tea and Christmas-cake Letty was uneasy as well as disappointed.

'Don't worry, Letty, my dear,' said Isadora, airily waving a teaspoon. 'There are a thousand reasons why he's been held up. Out there in the jungle the telephone cables are probably eaten by giant ants, and perhaps the wires are stolen by the locals to tie down their tin roofs.'

'It's not really jungle,' said Letty. 'There's a modern high-tech army out there you know. Jude's unit of UK sappers is under UN mission control. They must have all the latest satellites and whatnot.'

'That's all right then. He's simply queueing up to talk to Mum.'

Letty drank her tea, ate a slice of her own good Christmas-cake, and asked politely after Mrs Blum; but after Isadora had gone and she was sitting on the sofa waiting she was invaded by dismay. She breathed slowly and deeply, trying to relax. Active work in the garden was the cure for this anxiety, she knew, but it was already dark, and anyway she couldn't move far from the phone.

A mobile phone was what she needed now, she thought wryly, remembering how only last week she'd laughed at a young man feverishly using one as he walked along a crowded street. Music would calm her nerves, something quiet and orderly, something happy by Mozart. She sat down again after she'd fixed the CD, and began to listen to the Clarinet Quintet, thinking of the mischevious boy-genius with such a heavy load of work to carry, such a barrier of protocol to break through in order to achieve success, a happy, earth-fixed boy who caught glimpses of paradise.

The central heating turned itself off and the room grew cold long before she decided to go to bed, where she lay awake, alert and listening, but the phone remained unaccountably, cruelly silent.

She must have fallen asleep at last in the early hours of Boxing Day, and then slept soundly and late, till through thick wrappings of unconsciousness she became aware of a persistent knocking on the front door. She thought she could remember hearing a ringing of the bell too. Still feeling rather muddled she rose and put on a dressing-gown before running barefoot down the stairs.

She opened the door to a lean, grizzled man with firm features and steely blue eyes. Even in her sleepy state she recognized him as unmistakably a soldier, and thought of Schliemann's gold mask of Agamemnon, so like a British brigadier.

He held out a hand. 'Robert Bell,' he said. 'Lieutenant-Colonel. Am I speaking to Mrs Cresswell? Mrs Laetitia Cresswell?'

She nodded. He's come about Jude. Of course it must be. Oh God! Why would his senior officer call on her on Boxing Day? Oh God! Oh God! She dared not think, she dared not guess . . .

'It's about Captain Cresswell,' he said. 'Your son.'

A hand flew to her mouth, but terror stifled speech as she stood on the threshold trembling, and the blood drained away from her face.

'May I come in?' he asked. He stepped inside, and without a word Letty led him into the kitchen where they faced each other across the table. 'I'm afraid it's bad news,' he said.

'Is he dead?'

'Mercifully no. Not dead, but injured. An accident. Clearing mines. I don't know the details yet. There'll be an inquiry, of course.'

She was silent, as rigid in appearance and wooden as the back of the chair she was grasping.

'It happened on Christmas Eve, I understand, in Angola, where he is on a UN operation. There the buddy-buddy system would have got to work to give him first aid and a drip. That sort of thing you know. And then he was flown to Cyprus to Akrotiri – that's the RAF hospital on the British base out there – for major surgery. When he's got over that they'll fly him home, probably to the RN hospital, Haslar, in Portsmouth for any further surgery needed. For rehabilitation later he'll go to Headly Court in Surrey – the world's best for the job, I'm told. We'll let you know when that happens, of course.' When she still said not a word his manner and voice softened. 'We're all terribly sorry, Mrs Cresswell. We all think the world of Jude, you know. Such a good soldier. A rare breed nowadays. But he'll get the best treatment – the best surgery available, I can assure you.'

'Do sit down,' she said. 'Will you have coffee? I'm just going to brew some.' Life must go on. Small domestic rituals must fill the void, much-used phrases, like autumn leaves, must fall to cover dead ground where once spring flourished.

She looked down at her bare feet as she switched on the electric kettle, and glancing quickly at the disciplined man, sitting so spick and span at the table she realized she might seem to him a slut.

'I'm sorry I'm a bit dishevelled,' she said. 'I was fast asleep when I heard you knocking.'

'Of course. Boxing Day's a holiday, isn't it? Are you alone here?' he added. He looked at her feet, noticed that one of them was deformed, and quickly looked away again.

'Do you know what sort of injuries Jude has?' she asked. 'They're usually leg injuries, I believe.'

A delicious smell of fresh coffee filled the kitchen, cheering Lieutenant-Colonel Bell greatly. He'd had to make an early start that morning, and the light breakfast he'd eaten seemed very far away. He had undertaken on several previous occasions this sort of mission of direct personal contact with the wives or mothers of his men in order to give them bad news, and always dreaded it, more, he sometimes thought, than a barrage of machine-gun fire.

'I'm afraid we've received no details yet,' he said, 'but we do know that he has major injuries. And by the way, all arrangements will be made for you to visit him in hospital when he arrives back in this country. And we'll make sure there's somewhere for you to stay overnight, should you need to.'

'Thank you,' she said. 'The Army does look after its own, I've been told.' She put cups on the table, poured out coffee and sat down opposite him.

'Good coffee,' he said. 'Absolutely first class.' He drank it gratefully, thankful, too, that she hadn't turned out to be a hysterical woman, hadn't, amazingly, made any fuss at all. His steely blue eyes considered this Mrs Cresswell again. There was something appealing about her, something charmingly vulnerable, but she was brave, undoubtedly brave, gifted with that fortitude that women, he'd found, so often possessed.

She drank her coffee, watching him over the rim of her cup: the fatal messenger, bringer of bad tidings, who often in prehistoric times had to pay with his life for bringing them; but she was able to look at him without hatred because she hadn't really woken up to the meaning of it. She supposed she must be in a state of what was popularly called shock. What she'd been told was still beyond her grasp; it was unreal, not to be believed; it did not yet belong to her. In a little while, she thought, I will understand. I will know what's happened to him, what's happened to me. I don't know anything about it yet; I can't imagine it . . . . There was nothing now for her to do but stand by and wait, the two props of her standing being fear and hope, equally balanced. It was the lot of mothers since the beginning of human history.

8

That feeling of unreality, of living inside a glass bubble from where she could see but not touch the outside world, increased as she entered the echoing reception hall of the hospital. Interior design minimalist, white walls, green polished floor, white-coated receptionist seated, phone in hand, at a white counter on which stood a potted plant with dark shining leaves. A Sunday midday hush blanketed the building. The operating theatre was closed for the weekend, no busy surgeons with their white-coated acolytes were moving about the wards, patients had all been cleaned and tidied up and their beds straightened in readiness for visitors who seemed not yet to have arrived. Then a nurse in navy-blue uniform, summoned by phone, led her away along a corridor. The soft click and drag of Letty's uneven heels on the floor drummed through the white silence making her feel embarrassed as she walked towards the side-ward where Jude lay.

For a moment she wasn't sure of the identity of this patient smothered in bandages. The lower part of the face was uncovered, as was one eye, but this was shut. The left arm was strapped to the chest, but the right arm lay free across the bed. Tubing and a plastic bag containing some fluid hung on a stand at the bedside.

'Jude,' she said.

He opened his uncovered eye, looked at her, and then shut it again.

After a pause he said: 'I'm glad you've come.' It was Jude's voice. She clasped his free hand.

'Of course I've come. Are you in pain?'

'Not much. Doped up, I suppose.' After a moment he added 'Can't think clearly.'

'No need to think,' she said. 'Only to get well.'

His hand tightened round hers.

'What day is it?' he asked.

'Sunday.' Yes, it was Sunday, and Ben would by now have arrived at Number 11 Alexandra Terrace and found her gone. She had been unable to let him know what had happened, where she had to go, that she couldn't see him that day, couldn't see him again till heaven knew when. She had left him a note asking him to visit Barney, who would explain things; she had added love and kisses made of crosses.

'Was it awful? – out there?'

'Can't remember much. But yes . . .'

He sighed. 'Can't talk now.' After a long pause he said: 'Will you read to me like you used to?'

When he was a child he had liked adventure stories, Tintin cartoons, and science fiction, which she used to label boys' own fairytales. She looked at a pile of books on top of his locker, and wondered who in a busy hospital could find time to read to him. Surely not the nurses . . . She picked up the first book, *The*

Unicorn, by Iris Murdoch, and opening at chapter one began to read. Very soon she was seeing with the eyes of the young traveller, Marian, a strange, barren landscape at the furthest edge of Europe, pushing out into the Atlantic, of great limestone slabs intersected by tracts of bog and heather-tufted islands over which flew the hooded crows native to the west, sinister-looking birds like monks in buff-coloured habits with black hoods around their eyes, and black tails obscenely wagging as they walked. This desolate place was inhabited by the ghosts of neolithic peoples, the dolmens they had built, and the birds and wild flowers they had left behind.

"There are the cliffs."

Marian had read about the great cliffs of black sandstone. In the hazy light they seemed brownish now, receding in a series of huge buttresses as far as eye could see, striated, perpendicular, immensely lofty, descending sheer into a boiling white surge. It was the sea here which seemed black, mingling with the foam like ink with cream.'

The atmosphere of this ancient world, so far removed from the real one in which Letty normally lived and worked, seemed to echo her own feelings, smelt almost of the air she was breathing inside her glass bowl. Her strange state of being, she conjectured, must have been fashioned for her by nature as a protective coat, a sort of vacuum-packed anorak , in which to go into battle for the survival of her son. All her powers of love, hope and resilience must now be given to him. The surgeons had saved his life; but it would be for her to bring him back through many months of patient work, of repeated efforts and encouraging words, of slow climbing along a dark, narrow passage of many days towards a little sunlight, some small relief beyond, and hopefully to health and sanity.

It was impossible to know how much of the book Jude was absorbing, he lay so still with that one eye closed as she read on and the narrative unfolded, as fey a tale, she thought, as any science fiction, till he spoke suddenly:

'It must be an eerie country. Like going to the moon almost. Maybe I'll go west when I get out of here.'

'Yes,' she agreed. 'Yes.' It pleased her to think that in spite of his dreadful wounds he was already planning some sort of future.

Her reading was interrupted by a nurse bringing two cups of tea. Together they heaved Jude into a sitting position, and as they did so Letty saw the bedclothes subside into a hollow where his left leg should have been. The impact of this reality hit her like a blow across the face. She guessed the leg must have been amputated in Angola before he was put on the plane for home.

The nurse put the cup to Jude's lips. He sucked eagerly, but gave up the effort quickly, letting his head fall back against the pillows.

'It's too hot,' he said.

'We're going to get a new face tomorrow, aren't we Captain Cresswell?' the nurse reminded him cheerfully.

No reply.

The nurse met Letty's sudden look of fear across the bed. 'They're going to try a new synthetic skin for the graft,' she said. 'It leaves very little scarring.' Her voice was firm, reassuring.

'It's all right, nurse,' said Letty. 'I can give him his tea later. We'll let it cool a bit.'

She stood by the bed holding the cup to Jude's mouth after the nurse had gone. He drank slowly, savouring the taste.

'Good,' he said. 'That's good. I could do with another of those.'

'Have mine,' Letty offered.

'You sure?'

'Yes, of course, love. I can get one later.'

He drank it slowly.

'Bless you, mum,' he said. Then: 'One eye's not much good; but they've managed to save my sight in the other.'

'Thank God,' said Letty. 'That's something.'

'Something,' he agreed. 'They're going to operate again tomorrow, as you heard.' He shut his eye wearily.

Letty sat down beside him holding his free hand. His hold gradually loosened as he slipped down into a more comfortable position, and soon he was asleep.

Ben was waiting for Letty when she arrived home. He was sitting on the sofa in the front room, reading a Sunday newspaper and sipping a glass of her *Tio Pepe*, but as soon as he heard the front door open he leapt to his feet and ran out into the hall.

'Letty, darling, thank God you're back. Are you all right?'

She clung to him, hugging him desperately.

'I'm all right,' she said. 'It's Jude who isn't.'

He made her sit down beside him, he poured out a glass of *Tio Pepe* for her, which she didn't touch, he stroked her hand and let her tell him, stumbling over impressions and memories, about Jude, the hospital, and the operation to be done tomorrow.

'I shall ring the hospital of course,' she said, 'but I won't be able to visit him till the weekend.'

'I'll meet you at Waterloo,' he said, 'and we can travel down by train together. Celia will think I'm at St Augustine's. She doesn't know yet that I've stopped going there.' Inevitably she soon would.

Letty was thinking: This is the difference between a lover and a husband. In a crisis a lover can only help from afar; a husband is more than a Sunday comforter; he can take charge of things, smoothing out difficulties, sharing the strain, simply being there all the week. And now, since most of her weekends for the foreseeable future would be spent with Jude in hospital, Ben would be lacking even on Sundays.

'It's not going to be easy, Ben. Meeting, I mean . . .' she said.

'We'll find some way,' he said.

He would write to her; he would phone her from public phone boxes. She could write to him c/o LUMCA; it would be better not to phone him there except in an emergency. He usully spent most of Tuesday in London teaching a beginners' group the rudiments of organ-playing. Perhaps they could meet for lunch, or in a pub on Tuesday evenings? And perhaps another trip abroad together might be possible in the auntumn? He would love her always, dear Letty, always, always.

She clung to him, murmuring 'Always,' against the cloth of his jacket, knowing that events she could not control were sweeping them along, not knowing but fearing what the future held in store.

Jude . . . What would become of him, a young, athletic and hitherto energetic man now suddenly disabled and scarred for life? He had been such a beautiful little boy, and such a handsome young man. Oh, the pity of it, the *waste*! And as she wept Ben whispered: 'Letty, Letty,' kissing her hair.

Wayne found the front door and all the windows locked when he arrived, hoping for a tasty snack from Letty as she cooked her late breakfast on Sunday morning. He went round to the back of Alexandra Terrace where it was sometimes possible to effect an entrance, not across the barricades of barbed wire at the ends of gardens 10, 11 and 12, nor at No 8 where the old geezer, a woodwork nut, was always up early, sawing, hammering and planing in his garden shed and might spy him and give chase, but at No 9, where they slept late on Sundays. At the end of this plot there was a section of crumbling wall providing toeholds for Wayne to perch before swinging himself over on to the lawn; and getting into No 10 could be done by squeezing through a gap in the fence that Barney hadn't noticed yet.

'Couple of loose boards up there,' he explained to Barney, who was digging out the ripest portion of his compost and shovelling it into plastic sacks. Wayne stared at the steam rising from the hot heap into the cold air. 'Why's it so hot?' he demanded, and without waiting for a reply continued, jerking his head in the direction of No 11: 'Where's she at then?'

'She's at the hospital,' replied Barney. 'Visiting her son Jude, who's been blown up by a landmine.'

It took a few seconds for this momentous news to filter through Wayne's consciousness. He didn't feel sorry for Jude. Pity was not an emotion he'd known much of in his short life. Nor could he imagine Letty's feelings. Instead he saw a fast-moving film of war in the jungle, arrows of light streaking through darkness, cracks and explosions, a confusion of shouts, and Jude running through palm-trees, Jude lying injured, Jude glossed over with the blood of heroism and TV glamour.

'Hurt bad, is he?' he asked. There was sharp excitement in his voice.

'Come and give me a hand with this compost,' said Barney. 'And do something useful for a change.' And when the boy held open the mouth of a sack to receive the crumbly stuff he added: 'He's had a leg amputated, and he's lost one eye.'

'He'll have to wear a patch over it,' said Wayne. 'Black.' He thought he wouldn't mind wearing a black eye-patch himself. It would make people notice him; he would look different, and perhaps dangerous. Or he could wear black shades, like by Gucci, or Armani. That would be really cool. 'What's it like seeing with one eye?' he speculated.

'Not as good as seeing with two,' said Barney curtly.

Wayne peered into the sack to watch a knot of little pink worms wriggling.

'They don't half squirm, them worms,' he commented. 'What they doin' then?'

'Worms eat up all the leaves and grass we throw on this heap and pass it through their bodies, gradually turning it into soil,' Barney explained.

This surprising fact wound its way through the boy's brain as he stared at the worms.

'You mean all this stuff is worm-shit then?' he asked in disbelief.

'You could say that,' Barney admitted. 'It's good manure. If it wasn't for worms we wouldn't have much earth at all.'

Shock made Wayne let go of the sack as he voiced his feelings.

'D'you mean to say all the ground we walk on is just worm shit?'

'Not entirely. It's mixed with clay, and sand, and a bit of grit. There are some other creatures, too, germs and insects, which work on it. They're friends, not foes, worms,' Barney hastened to reassure him. 'If it wasn't for worms we wouldn't grow much food.'

Wayne stood up straight. 'Jude,' he said. 'Was he in a battle?'

'No. It was an accident.'

Letty had received a letter from her son's CO in Angola describing briefly what had happened. The mine had been touched off by something falling onto it. Jude was not in the process of defusing it when it exploded, but was standing a few feet away. Had he been stooping over it he would have been killed.

'It was a kind of landmine known as a Bouncing Betty,' said Barney.

When Wayne laughed Barney told him sharply to open the mouth of another sack and shut his own, and not till the boy was doing his job did he vouchsafe further information.

'Bouncing Betty's a nasty bitch of a mine,' he explained. 'She explodes on the ground when touched, and then jumps in the air before exploding again.' Millions of mines, he said, had been scattered over Angola during the long war. Nobody knew exactly where they all lay. Paths had been cleared and were mostly safe, but there were still mines, millions of them, lying about the countryside, hidden under bushes and stones and clumps of grass.

'It's the women and children who get blown up when they go out to dig the ground, and sow the seed for their crops, or to hunt for wild honey, which they like to make into some sort of beer, I've heard. That's when they get their feet and legs blown off.'

Wayne felt one of his own legs itching, and bent to scratch it. He did feel a kind of pity, then, for those unknown black children.

'Will Jude be coming home soon?' he asked, and added eagerly: 'He'll have an electric leg, won't he?'

Celia stood at the kitchen window gloomily watching snow descend. She was alone, and for once idle, having left Sarah and Chris at a children's party in Walnut Avenue. She had offered Ben the car that Sunday morning, since she herself would not be needing it to drive to Sussex, but he had refused the use of it, saying it was no picnic driving in snow, and he'd prefer to travel by rail. It had been a wise decision. The snow was really quite deep by now. She was wondering whether to risk going by car to pick up the kids after the party when the phone rang.

It was Father Gregory. 'Oh, is that you, Celia? I'm sorry to disturb your Sabbath peace with the clanging of telephone bells, but I wonder if I could have a word with Ben?'

'Isn't he with you at St Augustine's? He left this morning for Milton-on-the-Mount.' She had visions of a train crash in a blizzard, of Ben struggling along a twisted track through snowdrifts, Ben lying unconscious in a pile of nameless injured passengers.

'Oh no, no, my dear,' said Father Gregory. 'Sadly he no longer comes to us on Sundays. But it's not about today I want to talk to him. It's about a wedding. Full nuptial mass they're wanting. In a fortnight, with the Mendelssohn wedding-march of course. Everything laid on. It'll need rehearsing you see. And I'll have to get him here for that, busy as he is, I know.'

'I'll get him to ring you when he comes in,' she said.

She stood still for several minutes with the receiver still in her hand. So Ben wasn't going to St Augustine's on Sundays now. Where was he going, then? Celia's anxieties had gradually faded since her visit to Dr Corrigan. Least said soonest mended had been his prescription for marital ills; and she'd begun to believe he was right. No further mystery parcels arrived by post; life went on as usual. Ben maintained his regular timetable of work and relaxation, helped a bit in the house, and a bit more looking after the children; he didn't seem to be unduly unhappily married, and so she began to persuade herself that if he had been having that affair last year, it was probably over by now.

But suddenly here was this bombshell bursting into the once-more manageable routines of her life, and all her old suspicions, like pieces of shrapnel, fell back to hit her. Not only had she made a fool of herself in Father Gregory's eyes by showing that she had no idea of her husband's whereabouts, but she'd inadvertently let the cat out of the bag. Even Father Gregory's innocence, when later he remembered their conversation, would tumble to the fact that her husband had told her a lie that morning, would ask himself why, and inevitably a revelation of Ben's adultery would dawn on him.

She replaced the receiver with a bang. Well, she would have it out with Ben tonight. She wasn't going to be made a fool of any longer. She would attack him for his duplicity, telling him about Father Gregory's phone call and what even he must now suspect.

In fact Father Gregory suspected very little. Being celibate himself he was unaware of how much married people knew about each other's doings, and presumed Ben had forgotten to tell Celia about his change of routine. In any case his own thoughts were fully occupied by clefs and keys, by crescendos in sound and rallentandos in the speed of phrasing the great nuptial mass to be sung by his choir of twelve boys. Unruly rascals, too, some of them, especially young Prescott, who, though gifted by nature with a pure soprano and an exact ear, was inclined to race through his solo section in the *Agnus Dei*, not understanding perhaps that the Lamb of God was simply not for hustling. Any idea of his organist's being involved in such an untimely nuisance as an adulterous affair never crossed his mind.

Ben was late that night, so late that the children were in bed by the time he got home, cold and tired, with a few snowflakes melting on his black hair.

'Sorry Celia. I'm afraid you must have been worried.' Ben, who had been worried all day, but not about Celia, suddenly remembered her existence when he saw her grim expression as she sat at the kitchen table waiting for him.

'Of course I have. Worried sick. And now I suppose you'll tell me you were held up on the railway by snow on the line.'

'Well, yes,' he agreed lamely.

'Father Gregory phoned,' she said. 'He asked me to give you a message, as he wouldn't be seeing you today.' She paused to give greater dramatic effect to her words, hoping to enjoy his look of consternation as he realized he'd been found out. 'It seems you no longer go to St Augustine's on Sundays.'

Ben said nothing. What he'd feared was happening. He turned to hide his face and walked to the window, where he pulled aside one of the curtains to peer through the blackness, thinking: This is it now. The abyss beyond.

'I did tell you,' he reminded her, 'that my contract with St Augustine's was coming to an end. What did he want anyway?'

'He wanted to arrange a rehearsal with you for some big wedding up an the Mount.' But Celia was determined not to be put off. 'Where have you been all day, Ben?' she demanded. 'I want to know the truth.'

'I've been visiting a young soldier in a Hampshire hospital, who's been badly injured by a landmine in Angola, if you want to know.'

This unexpected answer took all the wind out of her sails.

'Why? Who?' she gasped. 'However did you get mixed up in this?'

'Tell you about it later, Celia,' he said. 'It's been rather a harrowing day as a matter of fact. Meanwhile I'd better ring Father Gregory.' He left the room, relieved that he'd won a brief respite in which to think.

Celia felt once more wrong-footed, conscience-stricken even, that she had so dreadfully misjudged him. But why didn't he tell her what he was up to, she wondered, as she hurriedly rose to warm up some soup for him, to serve it with bread and cheese and some mild apology for her unfriendly greeting. And Ben, swallowing his vegetable hot-pot, looked up at her anxious face across the table and relaxed into a smile.

'What would I do without you, Celia?' he asked. 'You are a real refuge in a storm.'

'Tell me about your Sunday's good deed,' she said, still with a little wary sarcasm.

'You remember last summer when I sprained my ankle on my way back to the station at Milton-on-the-Mount?' He spoke slowly, weighing his words. 'It was pouring with rain, and I couldn't walk, so I took refuge in the nearest house. I told you all that at the time.'

'Yes.'

'Well it was a young soldier who let me in, lifted me bodily over the threshold, and phoned for a taxi. Jude. I called there on my way home once or twice to thank him afterwards, and we became acquainted – well, friends really, over the odd cup of tea. And then he told me he'd been promoted. Captain Cresswell was going to Angola to clear landmines.'

'And then?' Celia was eagerly attentive.

'I heard no more about him till quite recently, when I heard he'd been badly injured.' He paused for a second. 'Father Gregory told me about the hospital.'

An image of his father swung suddenly across his mind's eye. He was standing in the backyard in his mechanic's overalls, paint-brush in hand because he was repainting a bedroom chair for Mother, while Ben was angrily inventing excuses, trying to cover up some childish misdeed with still more childish camouflage. He looked at his son's flushed face and said: 'A lie needs many legs you know.' Ben could still see the white paint dripping from his brush on to his overalls.

'What a dreadful thing to happen to the poor young man!' said Celia.

Thus began a period in his life which later he looked back on as the era of positive deceit. Before that he had managed to deceive Celia without actually lying; and as he believed she was quite unaware of his having forsaken her (except in so far as she was the mother of his children, and still held in her possession most of his worldly goods) he was able to persuade himself that he was not hurting her. So where was the harm in that state of deceit which was no more than a small economy with the truth? If she knew *that* she *would* be hurt. Chiefly in wounded pride, he told himself, as she couldn't really love him much, could she?

But once lies had been told it seemed to become more and more difficult to keep her happily deceived; and as the days passed and Ben was meeting Letty more frequently but not always on a Sunday, he found himself adding occasionally a not quite accurate detail to give the necessary touch of realism to his growing edifice of lies.

It was irksome, and quite foreign to his nature to be continually on guard about what he said at home, not only to Celia herself but to the kids, for fear of what they might innocently repeat, to remember carefully what he *had* said, and what he'd left unsaid.

His old man had been right all those years ago, he reflected ruefully, an alibi does need a lot of propping up.

9

As soon as he had played the last triumphant chords of the wedding-march Ben moved into the cheerful see-them-off mode of Widor's Toccata. It was quite a challenge to keep up the fast tempo demanded by the composer without slipping into errors, especially as a lot of footwork was required, and it was some time before the church emptied and he was able to fold away his music and descend from the organ loft to the church door. There, in spite of a cold January wind, bride, groom, bridesmaids and their families were grouped, shivering, but bravely smiling for the photographer. Most of the guests were drifting back to their cars as Ben moved unobtrusively through the thinning crowd. He was later than he'd anticipated, but he had booked a table for lunch at Toni's, and he knew Toni would look after Letty if she arrived before he did.

Toni greeted Letty with smiles and outstretched welcoming hands. He was pleased to see her. Very, very happy, yes. It was a long time, no? He led her to the table with a window overlooking the common. He couldn't help noticing some changes in her as he poured her out an aperitif. Poor little lady, she was tired, hollow-eyed, her movements had lost a little spring. She was sad; and Toni's warm heart and feeding talents longed to embrace and comfort her.

She seemed absent-minded as she sipped, gazing out of the window at the expanse of land empty of commoners apart from a few joggers on this cold day. Toni, hovering near her, flicked an imaginary crumb off the table with a starched white napkin and thought: Her mind is far off.

When Ben arrived and sat down opposite Letty Toni watched him closely, thinking: He too has the mind far off. There was trouble at this table. It was not a lovers' quarrel, he could tell, though he was old enough to know there was no love without some trouble. This must be the bitch Bad Luck; and her scratches must be endured, since there's no cure for them, only a little kindness.

He showed Ben the menu. 'The osso buco, with saffron rice is today especial,' he suggested gently. 'And the gremolata sauce has big aroma! Is from heaven!'

He kissed two fingers into the air. Then he fetched a bottle of his best Pinot Grigio and poured the wine solicitously into their glasses.

'Only one glass for me, Toni,' said Ben. 'Today I'm driving.'

Letty began to relax, and then to smile as Ben, doing his utmost to divert and cheer her, gossiped about the wedding, the nuptial mass, one or two anxiety-causing hiccups in the Introit but a perfect passage by young Prescott through the *Agnus Dei*, and then he made her laugh by his attempts to describe, stumbling in his ignorance of fashion trends, the garments of some of the more glamorous guests.

'What did the bride wear for this cold winter wedding?' asked Letty.

'A very modest dress,' he said, doing his best to recall the details. 'It was, I believe, velvet. A sort of ivory colour, with white fur at the neck and wrists, and a white fur hat instead of a veil. She should have had a fall of snow and a horse-drawn sleigh to carry her off on her honeymoon.' He finished his glass of wine. 'I haven't got a sleigh for you, Letty love, and no snow is forecast, but I've got the car, and I thought we might drive out into the country for a breath of fresh air.'

Letty could see plenty of fresh air blowing icily over the grass on the common, but she smiled and said:

'That would be lovely, Ben.'

It was late afternoon and the light beginning to fade by the time they got to Windsor Great Park; but they were able to walk there, admiring the trees, the oaks with branches densely curled and twisted like the hair on African heads, their shapes majestic in their leafless state. The coldness of the day had prevented many visitors from invading the place, and the few began to leave as twilight fell, so that Ben and Letty, almost alone in that empty space and silence, felt a new sense of peace and freedom. Soon the long green vistas of ancient trees and the steady movement of walking combined to quieten Letty's mind and heart, and though nothing in her life was altered by this afternoon, she began to think she might be able to cope with what was to come, with all the difficulties she could so vividly foresee.

'I don't think he'll be out of hospital for another month, perhaps more,' she said, as she climbed back into the car. 'But then he'll come home to me.'

They drove home in silence through the dark, and then sat quietly together drinking tea in the kitchen. Ben chose a CD and turned on the player.

'I've always wondered why you keep it in the hall,' he said. 'It's so likely to get nicked. Anyone who comes to the door can see it there.'

'I like music to fill the house,' she said, 'to circulate through the air like central heating. If I were to keep it in the sitting-room I wouldn't hear it in the kitchen when I'm working here.'

She sat at the table, warming both her hands around her cup. He stooped to kiss the back of her neck, and then stood holding her shoulders as Mendelssohn's *Hebrides Overture* flooded over them, sweeping them away in a rapid sunlit stream into the enchanted waters of Fingal's Cave.

'This was what was playing that first Sunday, when you came downstairs in your green mermaid suit. That was the first time I took you to Toni's. I think I fell in love with you in Fingal's Cave.'

'Was it? I'd forgotten.' She leaned back in her chair and smiled up at him. 'Dear Ben!' She put her arms round his neck and pulled him down to kiss his lips. She clung to him then, feeling in desperate need of love.

He stayed with her late that night. He knew she wanted to talk about Jude, about her anxieties and fears of proving an inadequate nurse and counsellor, and her dread of what the future had in store, so he held her long and lovingly, hoping that his arms about her might give her at least the illusion of that strength she was going to need.

'Do you think it will be like looking after a child all over again?' she asked.

'How helpless will he be?'

'I don't know yet.'

'He's a soldier, love. He'll struggle to be independent. Bound to.'

'But what sort of independent life can he look forward to? He's so disabled, Ben. And disfigured too.'

'You're imagining the future, thinking no woman will look at him?' He stroked her cheek. 'You're forgetting the compassionate woman, Letty. There are always a few of them about you know.'

'And supposing he comes home angry and full of hatred? That's what I fear most: that he may be terribly embittered by this experience.'

He stroked her hair, tangled and spread out on the pillow, like a net, he thought, to catch his soul; he reminded her that she herself had suffered a partial paralysis from poliomyelitis, and had survived it without growing exceptionally nasty, so perhaps her son would too.

'I was a child when it happened, Ben,' she objected. 'Children accept and make the best of things. They don't know any other possibilities. He's a young man in the prime of his physical powers. And his youth has suddenly been snatched away from him.'

'Well, perhaps he's still enough of a child to take it like a child,' he suggested. 'Perhaps he's brave, too, like his mother.' He kissed her gently; but Letty, suddenly aware of the passing of time, pushed him away.

'Is it all right, Ben?' she cried in alarm. 'So late? How will you explain it to Celia?'

'That's not your worry, love. That's mine. I'll think of something. But you're right. I must get moving.' And he rose and began to dress quickly.

Isadora squared her shoulders, threw her scarves around her neck, and tottered down the garden path on her high heels. She had to talk to Barney. He was busy planting his new potatoes, and saw her coming, but he didn't look up.

She decided not to beat about the bush.

'Did you notice how worn she looked today?' she demanded.

'You should wear a cardigan, Isadora,' he said. 'Those scarves are much too flimsy a covering in this weather. It's not even Easter yet.'

She ignored this advice, but continued to express her own line of thinking.

'It's all too big a trouble for her. You must know that. So don't try to avoid the subject. And that Ben – he's no help to her, battening on her, increasing her load to breaking point.' She glared at Barney, who said nothing, but continued earthing up his potatoes, for the tips of their first leaves were showing above ground. 'And how's it going to be when Jude comes home tomorrow? She won't be able to cope with him, and her job, and everything else as well. That Ben, he's not one of us, Barney, is he?'

Barney stood up and leaned on his hoe. 'But he may be one of hers,' he said. 'He's not a bad lot you know. No worse than the rest of us. We're all a patchwork of good and bad, with every living thing fighting for a toehold in the sun, and when one is crushed another takes its place. That's the sum of it. You can't do much about it.'

'What happens to the wounded, Barney? There are so many of them.'

'They fall out. And they'd wither and disappear, given time, if it wasn't for the likes of Letty.'

'It's her job to make things tolerable for them – for some of them – Jude for instance.'

'For the lucky few,' he agreed. 'The survivors.'

Isadora could see there was no help coming from that quarter, so she lifted her chin and sniffed.

'I don't think you understand the situation at all.' It made her angry to think of all the demands being made of Letty, who was after all the only wage-earner in their family of three – four, if you allowed for Jude, who, she knew must now be admitted to their three-cornered commune. He was Letty's son, and would contribute something to it when he turned it into a quad. The Army looks after its own, they said, and Jude would undoubtedly be given a desk-job in administration, or some such department, once he was patched up and rendered mobile. But Ben was nothing but a parasite, who had snatched away their lovely Sunday family lunches, and stolen most of Letty's love and attention. He did *not* belong.

She lowered her eyelids at Barney with an expression of extreme scorn. Men, she thought, see only what is in front of them; they don't see round corners as women can. She gathered her scarves around her and without another word turned and walked back to her own house. Here she threw off her shoes in the hall and padded towards the kitchen.

Her steps were slow and thoughtful as she made a pot of tea and carried it to the bay window of her sitting-room. She sat down, lit a cigarette, and with great satisfaction inhaled deeply. As she blew the smoke out of her nostrils she gazed beyond her barricades towards Chaplin Walk to make sure no invaders were on the move. This was the time of year they became active.

Her thoughts returned to Ben with a brooding animosity. *He* was the real interloper. In the long run, she believed, Letty would be glad to be rid of him.

Certainly Jude wasn't going to welcome him into their home. He would be jealous and resent his presence there.

Isadora remembered that other brief affair of Letty's, several years ago now – that freelance lover – what was his name? Divers, or Rivers, or some such fluid registration. Used to call himself Div, or Riv. Jude had hated him. And no wonder, since he had taken Jude's camera with him when he'd flowed on. It occurred to Isadora that Jude might be inclined to hate Ben too, might even be persuaded to help push out this cuckoo in the nest. But she would have to wait and see how the land lay in that direction. Meanwhile she must concentrate on the other person in this drama, Ben's wife, Celia Fording, the brisk voice on the telephone.

It was strange that there had been no response whatever to those early warning messages she had sent. Did Ben know about them? If so, he had won the first round in this duel between them. She would have to redesign her strategy. This Celia with the brisk voice, what sort of woman was she? She hadn't made much effort to discover the source of those messages. Had they not been clear enough for her to understand? That might be the case if the woman was stupid; but what if she didn't want to understand, was wilfully blind?

Between deep draughts of nicotine Isadora tried to imagine Celia's feelings and desires. It might have suited her to put up with things and say nothing. If she'd wanted a divorce she would have made a fuss. She probably couldn't afford divorce, whatever her personal feelings towards Ben. He certainly couldn't. They were both teachers, weren't they? Not high earners, even with the additional income from his organ-playing. And there were young children to make divorce more difficult.

In order to get this Celia to make a move it might be necessary to make her so angry that she threw prudence to the winds, lost her temper, and threatened Ben with the loss of his children. That, Isadora guessed, was where he was most vulnerable: his mistress weighed in the balance against his children. But what if Ben lost all common sense too, and agreed to divorce? What would happen then? That, Isadora decided, would leave them all in an even worse predicament, as Ben would have to move into No 11 Alexandra Terrace. A four-cornered commune might be just feasible, a pentagon would be overcrowding.

She poured out a cup of tea and drank it, and looking again towards the barricades, narrowed her eyes. There was another option open to this woman Celia. It would be taking a risk of course, but it might be possible to push her into another chain of events. If she were to attack Letty . . . Letty, being the good, sweet, unselfish person she was, would be moved by seeing a suffering wife, all tears and reproaches, pleading for the health and happiness of her children – of his children – and might be persuaded to relinquish her lover. Indeed that would be the best thing for everybody. The greatest good of the greatest number was what we should all work for, wasn't it? And in time Letty would accept it and be glad of her decision.

Isadora stubbed out her cigarette and lit another. This Celia . . . her religion might forbid divorce. She was riddled with religion, if hints dropped by Letty were correct, so it should be easy enough to shock her into action. But how? she asked herself. Aye, there's the rub . . . .

Wayne was very disappointed to find that Jude had no dark shades, not even a black patch to cover his missing eye, and he had to watch very closely to make sure the left eye couldn't move with the right before being certain it was a glass one.

'Can you pull it out?' he asked at last.

'I can,' said Jude. 'And do so every day.'

'Let's have a look then. Inside I mean.'

There was a short silence. Jude wanted some lunch. Letty had arranged for Isadora to come in and get it for him, but he didn't want to be dependent on that old bag with her airs and graces. There were quite a lot of things he could now accomplish with his right hand aided by the stumps of his left fingers, but he couldn't hold a lighted match and turn the gas on, all with one hand, and he wanted to fry an egg.

'Tell you what,' he said. 'If you turn the gas on for me when I say "ready", I'll take the eye out and let you see the socket. After we've had our eggs on toast.'

'OK.'

Wayne was cutting up Jude's toast into pieces on his plate when Isadora let herself in by the back door and Jude, watching her scarves float and settle behind her, wondered how she could cook without singeing them.

'Hi, Isadora,' he said.

Glancing round the kitchen she accepted the situation immediately. She could see that Wayne might prove a very useful slave for Jude. Letty had obtained a couple of days' compassionate leave from the Inland Revenue office for Jude's release from hospital, but had had to return to work that morning, and so had asked her to pop in at midday to cook him some lunch. This was the first time Isadora had seen him since his homecoming from hospital. He didn't seem too bad; she had expected worse. The skin of the left side of his face was red and puckered, but you didn't notice it so much when he smiled and the glass eye was really a very good imitation.

'I've brought you a bottle of sherry,' she said.

'That *is* kind. Could you open it and pour us all a drink?'

'Not for Wayne! He's much too young.'

'It's OK,' said the boy. 'There's loads of orange juice.' He fetched a carton from the fridge and poured himself a mugful, which he drank standing up, staring at Isadora thoughtfully. 'Funny name you've got,' he said. 'Not or'nary, is it?'

'I'm named after Isadora Duncan, the great dancer,' she explained haughtily. 'Not a ballet dancer, you know. She did free expression.'

'What's that?'

'I'll show you.' Isadora threw off her high-heeled shoes and, accompanying herself with her own soprano rendering of Rimsky-Korsakov's *Hindu Love Song*, which was, she thought, more or less in keeping with the great dancer's era, but which came out of her mouth as a high-pitched wail, she began to dance. She was certainly no sylph, but she was still remarkably nimble on her feet. She took little running steps, twisting and shaking her scarves above her head as her fat body bent and writhed, rose and shuddered, and her chins shook. She paused for a second, surprised by the outburst of laughter and clapping that greeted her performance. It was in her estimation high art, not music-hall comedy, but she was nothing if not an actress, and appreciation and applause being what they are, were not to be sneezed at, even if misplaced. She smiled and bowed, and sat down to recover her breath.

'Them scarves!' said Wayne, and burst into renewed laughter.

'Well yes, those scarves . . .' said Isadora. 'They were – at least one scarf was – the death of her.'

'How so?' asked Jude.

'She loved cars, you see,' Isadora began the story of her namesake with relish. 'Fast, open cars. In the twenties cars had wheels with spokes, you know.' The dancer, laughing excitedly in anticipation of the high-speed thrills she was about to enjoy, had taken her seat beside the driver. As she sat down she threw around her shoulders the long, trailing scarf she always wore, but the end of it caught and became entangled in the rear wheel, and as her chauffeur accelerated the scarf pulled on her neck, tighter and tighter, till she was strangled.

'It never!' murmured Wayne, leaning forward to feel one of Isadora's scarves, and wondering if hers were strong enough to strangle her.

She pulled it away from him crossly, angered less by him than by her own thoughts of Isadora Duncan's last years, how she'd come down in the world from her image of romantic glamour to a pitiable figure, her lovers and husband gone, her two children drowned in a tragic accident, and she herself old, fat and often drunk.

She turned to Jude. 'Letty said you'd be going to physiotherapy and rehabilitation tomorrow,' she said.

'Someone's going to pick me up in a car and take me there,' he said. 'They want to teach me how to manage ordinary everyday things with what's left of my hands before they teach me the computer skills.'

'I'm sure you'll learn very quickly.' Isadora smiled. A time would come when Jude would be fully rehabilitated, with a desk job at the Ministry of Defence, and perhaps in time a flat of his own in London. He might even marry some woman who could look after him. Then Letty could be reclaimed, and once that interloper Ben had been dismissed, life at No 11 would return to normal, to the contentment, the cosy chats and lovely intimacy they had once shared.

It was not till after Isadora had left the kitchen that Wayne was allowed to see Jude's eye socket.

'Cor!' he breathed. This was the real thing, not a TV documentary, so real that he didn't think he could bring himself to touch it, even if Jude were to permit that. His inquisitive gaze wandered towards the trouserleg that covered Jude's 'electric' limb. 'Can I see that?' he asked. 'Is it – like, digital?'

Jude stood up, holding the edge of the table to steady himself.

'You come upstairs with me and help me unpack and tidy things in my bedroom,' he said, 'and I'll show you the works.' He walked jerkily towards the door. 'I can't manage stairs very well yet, so you'd better come up behind me.'

'OK boss. I'll catch you if you fall'.

Jude sat down on his bed. He was pleased that he had climbed the stairs successfully, but he could see he was becoming apprenticed to a strange trade with a queer coinage: the satisfaction of a boy's curiosity with snippets of horror in exchange for services rendered.

When it came to survival the good soldier had to make do with whatever came to hand, and here was this boy at a loose end during his Easter holidays. But he did wonder if he was giving a good enough return, or was it just exploitation?

'Put those books on the bookshelf, will you?'

Wayne lifted the books from the open suitcase on the floor and placed them on the shelf.

'And see that the spines are all facing towards you.'

Wayne looked puzzled, so Jude had to explain which side of

the book was its spine. 'And see they're not upside down,' he added.

Wayne wasn't listening. He had found a book by Roald Dahl, an old childhood favourite of Jude's, and was staring at the picture on the cover. ' "Fan – tas – tic – Mr – Fox",' he read out in jerks. 'Oh yeah! Fantastic!' He laughed.

To Jude this was manna from heaven. He remembered the boy could hardly read. That was something he could teach him: to read. In that way they'd both be learning to equip themselves for an uncertain future.

'Go on,' he said. 'What comes next?'

Wayne opened the book and saw a picture of a fox hiding behind a stable door with the shadow of the farmer and his gun beyond.

'Is 'e gonna shoot 'im?' he asked.

'Tell you what,' said Jude. 'You can be my reader, and in exchange I'll tell you stories about my fighting in Angola. Not all at once, mind! Would you like that?'

'Not 'alf!' Wayne looked tenderly down at the warrior sitting on the bed. He supposed that it must be difficult for Jude to read with only one eye. 'I could read the papers, like. The news an' all.'

'Sit down here, and try to read some of that story.' Wayne sat down, but was reluctant to open the book. He wanted to talk.

'Do you like fighting?' he asked timidly, afraid of a rebuff.

'There are some people still in the world who don't under-stand the advantages of law and order. They've only reached the carnivorous cat stage of evolution emotionally, and they're a danger to the rest of us. So they have to be put down. And that may mean war. Somebody's got to be ready to do it. I am. That's why I'm a soldier.'

Wayne sighed. He didn't understand what Jude was talking about, so he presumed he'd never be clever enough for soldiering himself, but he could hear in Jude's voice how important it was to him. So he opened the book and began to struggle with the words.

Barney was cynical when he heard about Jude's mission to enlighten the illiterate. He had brought in a couple of cans of beer to share with him and was standing at the sink straining liquid from cooked spinach for Letty as she prepared supper.

'People like that, the denizens of Chaplin Walk, don't want to learn. They don't understand the advantages of literacy.' He carried the drained spinach to the table.

'Don't underestimate the people of Chaplin Walk,' said Letty, sprinkling salt over the pasta. 'Chaplin himself came from the underclass of his times.'

'You underestimate the evil in them Letty, their tendency to wallow in the sty without ever looking up. There are many who haven't yet grasped the importance of the Ten Commandments as a basis for a good life.'

'Perhaps the Ten Commandments aren't so relevant to their lives,' suggested Jude. 'Perhaps we need some new commandments for the new century.'

'I don't see any new Moses in the offing. A Jefferson might do – if he turns up in time.'

'We might make a start,' came from Letty as she stirred a cheese sauce for her pasta. 'What about: Thou shalt worship the Earth and all that is thereon, its mountains, rivers, fields and woods, and all its seas.'

'Brilliant, Mum! But don't forget all its creatures therein and thereon! It must be: Thou shalt not destroy the land and all its creatures, nor pollute the air and all things that fly in it.' Jude finished his beer, and waving the empty can in the air declaimed: 'And thou shalt not exploit thy neighbour's need too much!'

'Nor steal excess profit from another's work!' was Barney's command as he banged his can triumphantly on the table.

But their new commandments did nothing to enlighten her own and Ben's problems, thought Letty, pouring cheese sauce over her dish.

10

On Easter Sunday the sky was clear, the sun bright, birds in hedges moved briskly about their annual business of nest-building and egg-laying, singing lustily as they did so. All the gardens of Bushbridge were suddenly alight with the green fire of spring, and bristling with renewed life, the temperature was surprisingly warm for the time of year, and the car was available. Celia had not taken it down to Sussex for the holiday weekend because her parents were away on a Mediterranean cruise.

'What about an expedition, troops?' asked Ben at breakfast. 'Where would you like to go?'

'Sherwood Forest,' said Chris. He had been reading about Robin Hood and his merry men living under the greenwood tree.

'Traffic shouldn't be too heavy today,' said Celia. 'Weekenders have left London, and won't be returning till tomorrow. Somewhere in the Chiltern Hills? Beech woods there. But we'll have to get a move on.'

Beech woods in spring . . . Ben remembered walking in those

woodland cathedrals with his father years ago, the tall smooth columns of shining bark splitting high above their heads into a vaulting of palest green gilded by sunlight. Large areas had been felled, he knew, but there must be a lot of woodland still standing.

'I believe there are still some deer about, Chris. You might be lucky and catch sight of one.'

When at last they got there Chris ran about wildly, demanding: 'Where are the deer? I want to shoot them!' He had brought his bow and arrows for that purpose. But Sarah stood thoughtfully at the base of an old tree and, looking upwards, stroked the silky surface of its great trunk. 'Im-mense!' she murmured.

Ben and Celia watched her for a moment before exchanging smiles. Then Ben found a path and strode forward, carrying the picnic in his rucksack, while Celia lagged behind keeping a watchful eye on Chris as he darted here and there, hiding behind trees in order to take aim at his imaginary quarry, or to jump out and startle his mother with war cries.

The second movement of Beethoven's *Emperor* concerto was pursuing its course through Ben's head as he walked. He was thinking of Celia, how beautiful her hair used to be, and how he'd once thought of her as Cecilia, patron saint of musicians, to whom he owed a debt of gratitude if indeed, as legend would have it, she had invented the organ. She may have played the organ, and sung like an angel too, but poor Cecilia came to a sticky end. For dedicating her virginity to God, and persisting to the last in proclaiming her Christian faith, she was boiled alive in oil, but obstinately continued singing hymns throughout her immersion in the hot tub till her head was cut off.

It was an ignominious martyrdom that his own Celia was

unlikely to suffer. In any case she couldn't sing, being tone deaf. But he did sometimes have qualms of conscience about the possibility of his infidelity causing her pain. He stopped to look back, and saw her chasing Chris and laughing as she caught him. She didn't seem at all unhappy. If anyone was suffering in this affair it was he.

He wasn't sleeping well these days; he had bad dreams. Last night he dreamed he was swimming in the sea. He was struggling to keep afloat; he was rescuing someone from drowning, a woman, doing his best to keep her head and his own above water. Her long hair swirled about his wrists like slippery seaweed; he was losing his grip on the body he was holding as it changed into something else, some strange sea-creature, formless, unrecognizable. Someone uttered a cry of pain, and he woke with a feeling of horror because he knew he was losing Letty. He couldn't hold her body any longer as she drifted away from him on the stronger current of her other love. It was he who had been forced to cry out. But no. He made up his mind. He would not, would not let her go.

He could see ahead of him a clearing, a lovely little glade, and rippling through it a stream with hart's-tongue ferns hanging over the banks, with wood anemones scattered like star-dust all around. And there she stood in his mind's eye, not the elusive fawn of Chris's would-be hunting, but Letty the enchantress in her sweet nakedness, beckoning him into the dappled shade and sunlight of this spellbound woodland garden, offering him all that in his secret fantasies he had longed for. She was Debussy's *La Fille aux Cheveux de Lin*, she was Puccini's Butterfly whom he would not betray, she was Eve offering him the scarlet apple in whose juicy flesh was hidden the answer to all the perplexing questions he had ever asked himself. Oh, Letty, Letty, my heart's jewel . . . .

He stood stock still for a moment listening to the piano playing in his memory's ear. In the end you came back to Beethoven, his music so full of anguish resolved, rich in melodies of joy and longing, and all so securely balanced, the whole at last so satisfyingly *solid*.

Ben was a long way ahead of the others, and had to shout several times to attract their attention to the place he'd found. Sarah was the first to catch up with him. She had been searching for fungi growing under the roots of trees, and had filled the pockets of her anorak with broken bits of chanterelles.

'What about bivouacking here, Sarah?' he suggested. 'Seems a good place for a picnic.'

'What's bivouacking?' she asked.

Ben poured out two glasses of Wine Society claret before sitting down in front of the telly in Celia's study. He called out to tell her the nine o'clock news was about to begin. He could hear the children's voices echoing from the bathroom upstairs as with much fooling and as many delays as possible they put themselves to bed. Later he would go up and read to Chris.

Celia came in, and as she passed him she placed a hand on his shoulder. He caught it and gave it a little squeeze before she sat down.

'The kids have had a lovely day,' he said.

She sipped her wine murmuring: 'Mm, mm . . . that's good! And yes. They're great kids. We're lucky really, aren't we?' Looking at him sideways as he watched on the screen his favourite BBC announcer, the beautiful black girl with the good hair-do and the perfect broadcasting manner, who always seemed to be on duty on bank-holidays, she thought: It's been a nice, a very nice day. Perhaps, after all, everything's going to be all right.

At Whitsun she received the first anonymous letter. It arrived with a whole lot of advertising junk-mail that she threw straight into the bin. She was about to condemn the letter to the same fate when she gave it a second look, and paused. It was type-writen in an old-fashioned, slightly damaged type, and the postmark was legible: Milton-on-the-Mount. It was silly to be frightened by a piece of paper, she knew, but something about that letter made her hands tremble as she tore open the enve-lope. There was a single sheet inside, and it was almost blank, but typed in the middle of it in capitals with many smudged edges were the words: HAMLET. *ACT* 3. SCENE 4. LINES 183 – 187. There was no threat in that, nothing to be afraid of, but what on earth did it mean?

She had to wait till the holiday was over and school began again before she was able to go into the college library to find out. It was not an unusual thing to do, to pick up a book in the library during the lunch-break, but her heart beat very fast and her hands trembled as she feverishly searched the shelves. English Literature. Shakespeare. Collected Works of. Plays. She carried the book to a table and sat down to turn over the pages. *A Midsummer Night's Dream, Twelfth Night, Macbeth, The Merchant of Venice* . . . There were a lot of plays before she came to *Hamlet*, but there at last it was: Act 3. Scene 4. She counted the lines carefully with a forefinger. It was the scene where Hamlet, sickened by what he sees as his mother's adultery, and worse, as incest with his father's brother, scolds Gertrude for having married her brother-in-law so soon after his father's death. Celia ignored all the speech before and after the text she wanted: Lines 183–187. They jumped at her from the page. She read them over three times with intense concentration, and each time the words seemed to burn her eyes.

> *Pinch wanton on your cheek, call you his mouse,*
> *And let him for a pair of reechy kisses,*
> *Or paddling in your neck with his damned fingers*
> *Make you to travel all this matter out,*
> *That I essentially am not in madness.*

She shut the book quickly. The image was disgusting. I must keep calm. Filthy really. I will breathe deeply to steady my nerves. He is not mad, he, she, whoever sent that letter, even if it *was* typed on a crazy old typewriter, not mad. Wasn't that what he/she was trying to tell her: to listen to the message? Someone was romping in an adulterous bed. It cracked all her defences open, it made her suddenly fall prey to suspicions and anxieties, but it didn't get her very far towards learning the facts. *She* was not committing adultery. Someone was, but who?

Well, of course it must be Ben. He was the obvious candidate for the job; but who was he doing it with? Someone in Milton-on-the-Mount presumably, since the letter-writer posted the letter there, and perhaps lived close enough to what was going on to know about it. She was thrown back once more to her state of mind of last autumn, to feelings of paranoia about flower-arrangers at St Augustine's, and waitresses at the restaurant where Ben used to go for lunch after his sessions at the church. But he didn't go there any more, hadn't played the organ there since that big wedding in January. He was home very late that night, she remembered. She had wondered then what he'd been up to. But lately he had spent more time at home, more Sundays with the family, and she had been reassured, hopeful even. Perhaps the anonymous letter-writer might be essentially in madness after all.

Celia replaced the book in its proper place on the right shelf, and went into the cafeteria to get some lunch.

For a week she was beseiged by devils, swung on the torturing pendulum of jealousy between suspicion with hatred and disbelief with hope. When at breakfast she lifted her eyes from her bowl of muesli and semi-skimmed milk to see Ben opposite contentedly eating his, surges of rage bubbled up inside her like lava erupting from a volcano. Deceiver! Liar! *Paddling in her neck with his damned fingers* . . . Adulterer! O whited sepulchre! *A pair of reechy kisses* . . . What exactly did 'reechy' mean? The word did not spell loving kindness; it conveyed a reek of beer and lust and halitosis. Her spoon fell clattering on her bowl, and she rose from the table, unable to finish her breakfast.

Ben looked up. 'Are you all right Celia?'

Yes, surprisingly she was all right. She was still in control of the situation, and would remain so as long as no violent storm of words blew up between them. She had to be careful. Once certain things are said there is no going back; in every quarrel there is a territory that is the last crossing. She had to think it all out. She must be sure of all her facts. Hamlet's relations thought him mad; this anonymous letter-writer is trying to persuade me that he/she isn't; but perhaps he/she is some crazy nut, with peculiar sexual perversions. She didn't for a moment doubt that it was the same person who, last year, had sent her that horrible

165

corkscrew. It must be somebody in some way connected with St Augustine's, someone jealous of Ben's musical talents or his position there, or of his friendship with Father Gregory, or some other character from the school. In this way she built up an acceptable collage to explain to herself this beastly business. It was also a fence preventing herself from making any drastic move that might pitch her into irretrievable disaster.

When the second anonymous letter arrived she recognized immediately the smudged uneven letters of the unknown typewriter. She put the envelope unopened in her pocket to await some time later in the day when she would be safely alone to read its contents. She found them puzzling when she did.

> Don't look across the water.
> Thriving on English ground
> Named for a King's daughter
> The mustard can be found.

She folded the paper and put it in her pocket with some relief. The person who had written that was obviously mentally deranged. There was some rhyme in it, but certainly no reason. What disjointed notions were going through the poor creature's brain? Mustard called after a king's daughter ... ! And she mustn't look across some stretch of water, sea, lake or river, or whatever!

But the heart has reasons that reason knows nothing of, as Pascal has famously written; and her brain, under the influence of its instinctive drives, and in its silent ticking over of data, decoding and storing it by night, woke her with a start early one morning to remind her that Ben had once told her that the soldier who was injured by a landmine in Angola was Captain Cresswell. Cress was the clue. Mustard and cress.

She got out of bed and pulled the still-folded letter from her pocket to read it over again. Grows well . . . thriving on English ground. Could the water be the Channel? She didn't need to look across the Channel. Hamlet, Prince of Denmark. Elsinore was where Hamlet went, and that was in Denmark, wasn't it? With a sinking heart she remembered Ben's recent talk of a possible visit to somewhere in Denmark in September to examine pupils for LUMCA. He had even made a joke about the possibility of visiting his father's ghost in Elsinore.

She slipped a dressing-gown over her nightdress and crept downstairs very quietly. She didn't want to wake anybody. She found the telephone directory and turned the pages over till she came to C. Cameron, Chapell, Connell, Craven, Cresswell. There weren't many Cresswells; but there was one in Milton-on-the-Mount. L. Cresswell. There was no indication that L. Cresswell was a captain. Briefly, she wondered what that L stood for. Lawrence, Leonard, Lionel? The directory didn't say. Perhaps L was the father of the captain, but there might be a sister, or a wife living in the same house. His mother, she reckoned, would be too old , and unlikely to be carrying on an affair. Then her eye was caught, like a fish on a hook. There it was at last in print, in black on the white page, as clear as daylight now: 11 Alexandra Terrace: English ground named for a king's daughter. Alexandra, who married Edward VII, was the daughter of King Christian of Denmark. Celia knew that. She was the beautiful, noble, generous queen who accepted her husband's infidelities, who actually let Mrs Keppel in by the back stairs to sit with Edward when he was dying . . . ! But then she was married to a King-Emperor, and lived in palaces, and was painted by Sargent in black and wearing pearls. Ben was a music teacher and church organist, and lived in a heavily mortgaged house in the suburb of Bushbridge. And Celia certainly had no pearls.

So now she knew.

It was a kind of grim satisfaction, the end to all her doubting, but she felt bitterly humiliated, rather as if she'd been sacked from a job for inefficiency; and the most humiliating thing in all this affair was that she'd been such a fool not to see the truth months ago.

'I want you to look after the kids on Sunday, Ben,' she said. 'You can have the car, and take them out somewhere. I need the day to myself .'

'Sure,' he said. 'You doing anything special?'

'The old girls from my class at school are meeting in town for a celebration, and I'd rather like to join them. I can go up by train. I haven't seen any of them for years, you know.' Lying was sinful, but lies weren't mortal sins, only venial ones. And the end does sometimes justify the means.

On Sunday Jude was taken out by his physiotherapist for a drive in the country. She wasn't very young, being in her thirties, so Letty guessed when she arrived to pick him up, but she was lively and attractive as well as being muscular. Belinda was her name. Belinda gladly accepted a cup of coffee as she waited for Jude to come downstairs. When he opened the kitchen door he stood there, freshly shaved, his thick black hair sleek from brushing, his manner happily expectant, and smiled at her.

She, laughing, cried out: 'Hi there, Jude!'

It was obvious to Letty that powerful sexual vibes were passing between them. Belinda didn't seem to mind that the skin of his face was still red and raw from flash burns, and that his smile was lopsided. Isadora, who had dropped in for elevenses, met them in the hall as they were leaving; she felt the vibes too.

'It's all very satisfactory, Letty,' she said. 'All entirely as it should be.' She sat down on a kitchen chair and lit a cigarette.

'Oh, I'm delighted!' cried Letty. 'So happy for him! I only hope she's as nice as she looks. And even if it doesn't come to anything permanent it will give him confidence, make him think he can still pull the birds – to use his lingo.'

Isadora nodded.

'And isn't he lucky to meet her so soon after . . . after . . .?'

Isadora agreed. Things were certainly working in the right direction; but she reminded herself that hubris awaited the too complacent, and that even in well-regulated lives there were annoyances. The best laid plans of mice and men . . .

'Those bloody mice!' she exclaimed aloud. 'I'm being invaded by mice, Letty. I don't know where they're coming from. Probably Number 13. She lives in a perpetual mess, and never puts her dustbin out. Well, I've never seen it go out. What's more I can't catch the little beggars. They eat the cheese from my trap but don't leave their necks on the block.' She inhaled deeply. 'I intend getting a big, black, implacable, death-dealing cat.'

'Oh, the poor little mice!'

'You're seeing them with Beatrix Potter's eyes, Letty. Sweet little creatures dressed up in mob-caps and embroidered waistcoats. The Tailor of Gloucester stitching a tiny buttonhole with minuscule silk stitches, but dropping his nasty little black buttons all over the cups and saucers on my Welsh dresser, that I bought for a song years ago at the selling-up of a farmhouse. I believe that sale was in Gobowen. But it might have been Oswestry. Somewhere in that direction.'

'I suppose I am sentimental. I suppose if their numbers weren't kept down mice would take over the world, like rabbits in Australia.'

'Or like human beings in the Third World.'

Letty said nothing to that, but silently poured aromatic coffee into cups.

'Is Ben coming to lunch today?' asked Isadora.

'No. He's looking after his two children today, as his wife has to go somewhere else.' She sighed. 'I don't see him so often now, you know.' She sighed again. 'But I'm hoping we may be able to arrange another holiday, perhaps in September. It might be Denmark this time. There's a music school there, not in Copenhagen, but in some smaller town, which wants its pupils examined by LUMCA. And he thinks he'll be able to get that job.'

'That would be nice.' Isadora smiled, narrowing her eyes against the sting of her cigarette smoke.

Letty was standing at the sink scrubbing Cornish new potatoes for Sunday lunch when the front door bell rang.

'Oh hell!' she said, trying to dry her hands on her apron.

'Don't move, Letty dear,' said Isadora. 'I'll go and see who it is. It might be that brat Wayne.'

'No, it won't be him. He won't come today because he knows Jude's going out.'

Isadora opened the door to a strange woman who addressed her as Mrs Cresswell.

170

'I'm Celia Fording,' said the stranger.

It was the brisk voice all right. It had short cropped pepper-and-salt coloured hair attached to it, and a good deal of middle-aged spread below it.

'Come in,' said Isadora, altering her own voice by exaggerating its tobacco-dried huskiness. Things were really going well; it was almost too good to be true.

'I'm not Mrs Cresswell.' She waved her cigarette about. 'Letty's in the kitchen cooking lunch. It's Miss, by the way, not Mrs. Her son's been taken for a drive by the physiotherapist this morning.'

Celia stepped inside. She was not slow to take in this message. Letty was the L of the telephone directory. She must be the captain's mother, but a Miss. She was a single parent, and that sort of people did tend to fall from grace as teenagers, so she might be still quite young. Any small remaining doubts she felt about coming to this house were quashed, and her determination to send this woman packing was fortified by a fresh dollop of moral righteousness as she followed Isadora across the hall and into the sitting-room, where she stood waiting.

'Do sit down,' said Isadora. Then she went to the kitchen.

'It's Mrs Fording, Letty. I've put her in the sitting-room, as I daresay it's a formal visit.' She didn't hesitate on seeing Letty suddenly turn pale. 'I'll leave you two together. I must go down to Barney's to pick up the asparagus for lunch.' She was very calm, very satisfied. Everything was beginning to fall into its proper place.

Letty was far from calm. She was agitated, brushing down her hair with trembling fingers, fiddling with her apron-strings in an unsuccessful attempt to take the thing off.

'How on earth has she tracked me down?' she asked distractedly.

'Husbands do sometimes blab to their wives,' said Isadora, pursing her lips before exhaling. She couldn't help feeling a little triumph.

She shut the back door quietly, and stood for a moment in the porch, surveying the gardens spread out before her. Her damson-tree had flowered in a white avalanche two months ago, and was now forming little fruits; the buds of Letty's beautiful *Rosa Nevada* were beginning to open, and beyond it were Barney's vegetable beds all in good productive order. She smiled contentedly. . . . *This little world . . . this blessed plot, this earth, this realm, this England* . . . And there was Barney pottering happily in his greenhouse, the foolish man, utterly oblivious of the drama being enacted under his nose. There was no sign of tottering on her high heels as she sped down the garden path towards him. Men were awfully stupid about some things.

Letty entered her own sitting-room and waited for a torrent of abuse to be poured all over her. She dried her hands nervously on her apron. She didn't look at Celia, who was staring at her with increasing indignation and thinking: She looks extraordinarily young to have a son old enough to be an army captain. She must have been under age when she conceived. She wasn't all that pretty either, but she was – there was no doubt about it – she was the same person as that laughing girl in Ben's photo holding the toy octopus. The remembered image touched a sore place in Celia's feelings, and she felt a surge of hatred for this woman who stood meek and silent before her, still wearing her kitchen apron and her false humility! She could punch her face! But years of early conditioning in good manners held her in check, and she began her attack with a diplomatic spray of courtesy.

'I was sorry to hear about your son's injuries in Angola,' she said. 'He must be a very brave young man.' She did feel a tiny twinge of pity for the mother too.

'He's over the worst,' said Letty. 'Thank you.'

There was an awkward silence as Celia hesitated. 'I'm sorry to have to ask you this, Miss Cresswell, at such a time of trouble as I know you must be going through . . .'

'Yes.'

'But, well . . . are you my husband's mistress?'

'Yes.'

Celia had expected confrontation, not meekness, and was a bit taken aback, though of course in her professional life she was quite used to giving the occasional dressing-down to an idle and disruptive sixth-form pupil.

'I don't think you're a fool,' she said. 'You must know that you're going to break up a perfectly good family.' She paused. 'Adultery is easy,' she added bitterly. 'Keeping a family together is hard work.'

Letty was irritated by Celia's assumption of superiority.

'Adultery isn't as easy to commit as people seem to think,' she said.

Celia ignored that. 'Have you thought what divorce would do to Ben's children?'

'Of course, of course. Many times!'

'And if I divorced him he'd have no money, you know, no money at all, and no house, no music-room to do his teaching in, and probably no teaching either. Have you thought of that?'

Letty began to cry.

'I love him,' she said.

At that Celia's self-control snapped.

'Love!' she sneered. Even the none-too-clean and far from glamorous cook's apron Letty wore could not conceal the pretty throat rising above it, nor flatten the soft contour of her breasts beneath it. *Paddling in your neck with his damned fingers ...* The thought of it was so sickening it almost choked her, but she forced out her words in hot angry rushes:

'Love isn't selfish! Love thinks of the loved one's good. You don't! It's lust you feel for him. You're nothing but an old-fashioned common little whore!'

A red flush spread over Letty's face and neck. She raised her head, and took a step forward.

'And what sort of love do you have for him, may I ask?' Her voice rose angrily. 'You may be the mother of his children, and you may live under the same roof, but you've denied him sex for years. What sort of love is that? It's not a marriage at all; and you're no real wife! You're just trying to hang on to a tame breadwinner, that's all!'

For a moment Celia was shocked into silence. So Ben had been blabbing all sorts of intimate secrets of their married life to this – this woman? It was terribly humiliating. And of course this sort of woman could have no inkling of the reasons, the advantages of sleeping in separate rooms.

'No doubt sex is the only thing you ever think about,' she said at last. 'But there's a lot more to marriage than sex, you know.'

'Ben loves me,' said Letty obstinately, though she resisted the impulse to tell this hateful woman that Ben couldn't possibly love *her*.

Celia sat down quickly on the sofa. She zipped open her shoulder bag and took out a tissue which she crumpled into a ball and rubbed over the palms of her hands. She knew only too well that what Letty had just said was true.

'It won't last,' she said. 'These things never do. And if you're the cause of his losing his children he'll soon begin to hate you.'

Letty sat down in a chair opposite her. Tears collected in her eyes and slipped slowly down her cheeks and on to her hands folded in her lap. Celia stared at her rival, sitting there weeping steadily. She looked a sorry mess. Not a shred of glamour left; not much of a threat, you might think, but there was no accounting for other people's sexual preferences, even people whom you thought you knew quite well.

'I don't want you to divorce him,' Letty sobbed. 'I only want him on Sundays.'

There was a long, a very long silence. Something jolted inside Celia's brain. A sluicegate had suddenly opened to divert the flow of her thinking into a totally new channel. *Only on Sundays . . .?* That would be condoning adultery. But she herself wouldn't be committing it, and she couldn't be responsible for other people's sins. She wasn't her husband's keeper after all.

Slowly she zipped up her bag. Slowly she rose from the sofa. She walked to the door as if in a trance, and there she paused and looked back over her shoulder at Letty sitting with bowed head, still weeping. 'Only on Sundays . . .?' she murmured as she went out.